# ENTANGLED IN SCARLET

*Blood Oath #3*

## J.A. CARTER

*Blood Oath Series*
*Bound in Crimson*
*Tempted by Fire*
*Entangled in Scarlet*
*Fated in Ruby*
*Unraveled by Desire*

# BLURB

**They vowed to own me—body, heart, and soul. I never thought I'd let them.**

The only thing more terrifying than being taken captive by four vampires is falling for each of them. Despite their rocky start, Calla can't imagine her life without the immortals she's bound to.
And when they're attacked by vampire hunters, they have no choice but to run. While Calla struggles with another life-altering ambush, Kade faces his own in the form of his dead sister. They say the bonds of family are the strongest, but this reunion isn't a happy one.

As tensions rise between the vampires and hunters, extreme measures are taken by the oldest vampires in history to ensure the survival of their race. There isn't a moment to breathe before Calla is once again forced to acknowledge the deal her ancestors made for her life.

Until she discovers the consequences of the blood oath may not be *hers* to face…

*This one is for the readers who live for the sexual tension between Atlas and Calla.*

# KADE

eing stabbed hurts like a motherfucker.

Fire licks across my skin, radiating from where the dagger sticks out of my chest.

She missed my heart. Barely.

The sky above me is bright, and I squint at the sun, closing my eyes as the sound of Calla screaming rips through the air.

Everything happens in slow motion after that.

Atlas's sharp voice pushes past the fog gathering in my head. "Open your eyes, Kade."

I force them open, only for the world to spin. We're moving—toward the house, I think. My eyes close again; I can't keep them open.

My fangs cut into my bottom lip, and my stomach churns at the taste of my own blood, my head clouding with thoughts of death—the end of my immortal existence—and at the hand of my own sister.

*Meredith.*

Her name punches me in the gut, knocking the air out of my lungs.

She's alive. But how? Who made her a vampire, and why? Why didn't she come to me after it happened? What in the actual fuck was her reason for stabbing me at our reunion? So many questions and so much pain, I can't breathe.

I'm vaguely aware of Atlas setting me on the couch in the living room as he says something to Calla. It's too muffled for me to make out, but a moment later, he grips my shoulder, and white-hot pain explodes in my chest, filling my entire body as he pulls out the dagger, slamming it down on the coffee table.

I gasp loudly, my eyes flying open as I growl at him before I can stop myself.

"You're welcome," he mutters, his jaw set tight.

"Is he going to be okay?" Calla's voice is small and filled with fear. Atlas glances past me; Calla must be standing behind the couch, but everything still hurts too much for me to turn and look.

"The dagger missed his heart. He'll live but he needs blood."

The room is silent for a moment, replaced quickly by the sound of her footsteps moving away from the couch. When the next sound that reaches me is of her pulling a knife from the block in the kitchen, I force myself into a sitting position, gripping the back of the couch until my knuckles turn white. I peer down at my chest and grumble incoherently. This was one of my favorite shirts.

Calla walks back to the couch, swallowing hard as her pulse kicks up.

I eye the knife in her hand. "What are you doing?"

"Atlas said you need blood." Her voice is shaky but her grip is steady.

"There are bags of blood in the fridge in—"

"Fresh blood will heal you faster," Atlas chimes in.

"It's okay," Calla assures, perching on the couch next to me.

Atlas plucks the knife out of her hand, setting it next to the dagger, and Lex walks through the front door before Calla can say anything.

He looks downright pissed. "I fucking lost her." He focuses his gaze on me. "I'm sorry, brother."

I shrug, still in knots thinking about the target he was chasing. I haven't seen my sister in over a century, and after months of searching for someone who clearly didn't want to be found, the authorities gave up hope that she was alive. Weeks after that, our parents did too.

I need to know what happened. I need to find her and figure out what the hell went down the night she disappeared and the decades that followed. Our parents are long dead, and I've made my own family with Lex, Gabriel, and Atlas, but she's still my sister. Even if she wants nothing to do with me, I need some semblance of closure.

"You good?" Lex checks, glancing between me and the others.

"I'll live," I tell him before turning my attention to Calla. She immediately offers me her wrist, and I don't hesitate. I don't have the control to ease into it or be gentle. My fangs sink into her skin and the taste of her blood explodes on my tongue.

She winces, pressing her lips together, but doesn't pull away. Once my venom has a chance to reach her system, she relaxes, leaning against the back of the couch as a sigh escapes her lips and her eyes flutter shut. The sight sends blood straight to my cock, making it twitch in my pants. Despite almost dying at the hand of my supposed-to-be-dead sister, Calla still makes me fucking hard. It's kind of messed up, but I really don't have the strength to give a fuck right now.

"Kade," Atlas says in warning, and I notice the sound of Calla's heartbeat slowing.

I force myself to pull away and drag my tongue over the puncture marks to seal them.

She blinks her eyes open, smiling softly. "Better?"

I nod, leaning in to kiss her cheek. "Thank you."

Lex walks behind the couch, leaning against the back of it, and lets out a heavy sigh. "What in the actual fuck just happened?"

Despite the warmth of Calla's blood flowing through me, a shiver races down my spine, making my muscles tense. "That was Meredith." The sound of her name leaving my lips after all this time has nausea rippling through me, and I clench my jaw for a moment before I'm able to continue.

"I thought your sister was dead," Lex says, raking his fingers through his already messy white hair.

I blow out a breath, which does nothing to ease the pressure in my chest. "Yeah. So did I." Part of me wants to get off this couch and go after her. Lex couldn't find her after she fled, but maybe I can track her blood. We share the same DNA, so there's a chance I can find her. Though that begs the question of why I never felt her presence before. Excellent. Another fucking question that left unanswered is going to make my head explode soon.

Atlas gets up, walking to the kitchen and pouring a glass of orange juice, before coming back and sitting on the armrest. He tilts Calla's face up with a finger under her chin. "You need to drink this."

She blinks her eyes open and, surprisingly, takes the glass without protest and drinks until it's empty before handing it back to him.

"Good girl," Atlas says.

"Fuck off," she shoots back.

My lips twitch. *That's our girl.*

"What do we do now?" Calla asks, her brows pinching together with worry.

"Add this to our ever-growing list of problems," Lex offers, shrugging.

Without warning, the entire back wall of windows shatter. There isn't a moment to process what just happened before half a dozen men and women dressed in all-black uniforms flood into our home with vicious, hateful expressions and daggers raised to fight—to kill.

Goddamn vampire hunters. Now? *Really?*

They rush forward, but Atlas and Lex are faster.

"Get her out of here," Atlas barks over his shoulder, his fangs bared as he takes on a hunter. The man, who is at least a foot taller than Atlas snarls at him, swinging his fist toward the vampire's face. Atlas laughs harshly, catching the hunter's fist in his hand, and throws him backward, taking out two other hunters.

I'm already off the couch, hauling Calla up and shielding her with my body as we move toward the garage.

Lex smirks from where he's facing off with two female hunters, who apparently thought if they worked together they could take him out. Not likely.

"We can't leave them," Calla cries, her voice pitched high with fear. She tries to dig her heels into the floor to stop us, but I lift her easily and keep moving until we reach the door to the garage. "Kade!"

"They're right behind us. Chill the fuck out." I meet her brown, wide-eyed gaze and smirk. "Please."

She stops fighting me, but her heart is still beating rampantly in her chest.

"Everything is going to be fine," I tell her, pushing the garage door open, then pulling it shut behind us. I have no fucking clue if that's true, but the terror on her face is making me feel sick. I want to do whatever is necessary to make it go away.

The sounds of feet scuffling and bodies hitting the floor inside the house continues as we walk to the Escalade. My gums throb uncomfortably at the scent of human blood hanging in the air. I get Calla into the backseat and slam the door shut, climbing behind the wheel. Atlas's souped-up vehicle isn't my ride of choice, but it's the most practical at the moment. I glance at the bright red Maserati beside us and frown. There's a good chance I won't be able to come back for my baby, and that fucking sucks.

I turn the key in the ignition and start the car just as the door to the house opens and the guys jog toward us, their clothes spattered in blood. Atlas takes the passenger seat, while Lex climbs in the back with Calla.

"Drive," Atlas growls, staring forward.

I pull out of the spot without a word and hit the door opener before peeling out of the garage. Heaviness hangs in the car as we leave the house in the rearview; we all must know we're not coming back here, to the home we built.

We're barely past the Washington city limits when Lex gets on the phone to Marcel. He fills him in on the situation, though Marcel had already gotten a call from our security team notifying him of a breach in the system, they had no idea there had been an attack. The hunters must've overrode the tech; our team didn't even have a chance to move in before they attacked.

"I'll have a team go in and clean things up," Marcel tells Lex. "Keep moving. I'll text you the address to a safe house a few hours from you."

They end the call, and Lex sighs. "You got all that?" he checks with Atlas and me, and we both nod.

"Yeah, no. I don't have super hearing," Calla says. "Someone want to tell me what's going on?"

"We can't go back to the house now that the hunters know about it—about us."

Which begs the question of *how* they found out we're vampires. It doesn't make sense. We've lived for decades—for over a century—undetected by them. What the fuck happened?

"Right," Calla says with a frown I catch in the rearview mirror. "And what about that girl? Meredith?"

My grip on the steering wheel tightens, and I press the gas a little harder. "I had no idea she was alive... or that she had been turned. She, uh, disappeared from a party a long time ago, when we were both still human." I merge onto the interstate and speed up to get into the fast lane before continuing. "We searched for months, but once a certain period of time had passed, she was presumed dead." I swallow hard, surprised at the emotion clogging my throat after so long. "My family, we had a memorial service and buried an empty casket."

Calla sucks in a breath. "I'm so sorry." A moment later, she asks, "Why would she come after you after all this time? Or at all, for that matter?"

I keep my eyes on the road. "Before everything happened, we were very close. Her... her disappearance devastated me. I can honestly say I have no idea why she would try to kill me."

Atlas clears his throat. "Perhaps we should consider the possibility that her attack was a distraction for the hunters' ambush."

My stomach clenches at his words, at his assumption that Meredith could possibly be working with the hunters. I thought I knew her better than anyone else in the world, but I have to look at the facts here. I haven't seen or spoken to her in more than a human lifespan. I have to face the idea that I have no idea who she is now or what she's capable of.

"Well, fuck." Lex's voice is low, deepened with anger. "We now know of at least two vampires who are associated with the hunters."

"Wait. You think Selene had something to do with this too?" Calla asks.

"It really doesn't matter right now," Atlas says, glancing down when his phone chimes. Mine and Lex's do as well. "It's Marcel." Atlas plugs the address he sent us into the GPS built into the dash.

I glance at the map on the screen and sigh. We still have a little over three hours of driving to reach the safe house and decide on our next move.

"You want me to drive?" Atlas checks.

I shake my head automatically. "I'm good."

"Liar," Lex mutters from the back seat. "Pull over and let Atlas drive."

"I said—"

"Kade," Calla cuts in with a soft voice. "Please."

I meet her eyes in the mirror for a moment before letting out a low breath. "Fine." I flip the signal on and pull off to the shoulder, putting the car in park. Unbuckling my seat belt, I get out of the vehicle, pulling in a deep breath. The early afternoon air is warm for the middle of April, but it does nothing to combat the chill in my bones. I can't get Meredith's face out of my head. Or the burn of the dagger she plunged into my chest.

"Kade." Atlas's voice pulls me back, and I blink at him. He claps me on the shoulder. "Do you need a minute before we keep moving?"

I shake my head. "Let's just go." Walking around the front of the Escalade, I climb into the passenger seat and buckle up, staring out the windshield as Atlas gets behind the wheel and pulls back onto the interstate.

❧ 2 ❧

## CALLA

After dozing off a couple of hours into the drive, I come to, blinking my eyes open when I can no longer feel the car moving but instead feel the warmth of Lex's hand against my cheek. The sky outside the tinted windows is still light, and I glance at the clock on the dash—it's a little after five.

"We're here," he murmurs in a tired, soft voice. The darkness under his eyes makes me feel bad for sleeping.

I nod, reaching for my seat belt. Before I can open the door, Kade is out of the passenger seat and opening it for me, offering his hand. Accepting it, I let him help me out of the car, the gravel driveway crunching under my Doc Martens. I sway a little, still not fully awake, and he catches me easily, sliding an arm around my waist.

A quick glance around lets me know we're not in any type of large city. Aside from the small, single-level, white farmhouse up the driveway, there are only pine trees for as far as I can see, their muted green color matching the shutters on either side of the windows in the front of the house. The air is warm and fresh, the late afternoon sun beating down on us.

"Where are we?" I ask as we walk toward the place I imagine we'll be staying until we figure out what the hell happened back in Washington.

The wood steps up to the paint-chipped porch creak under us, and I cringe, trying to step lightly. The only modern thing about this place so far is the lock built into the faded blue door. It's a numbered touchpad that Atlas quickly keys the code into, opening the door.

"Somewhere safe," Lex answers from behind me and Kade. "It's temporary."

The door opens into a small foyer that smells of lemon and something a bit stronger, like some kind of cleaner. I was expecting the air to be heavy with dust and the stench of mothballs, so this is a pleasant surprise. Maybe Marcel had it cleaned while we were on our way here. The floor beneath our feet is a worn hardwood with a dull gray runner stretched along the length of the hallway before us. On the left side of the hall is a set of open double doors that lead into a living room, and on the right are a pair of closed wooden doors that I can guess are bedrooms.

I follow Lex and Atlas into the living room, which also leads to a small kitchen and dining area. This part of the house is surprisingly open-concept for how old I imagine it to be.

Lex drops onto the brown leather couch and lets out a deep sigh but says nothing.

I glance from him to Atlas, specifically to both of their bloodstained clothes. "I don't suppose this place comes stocked with food and clothes," I offer wryly.

Kade slides past me. "Food, probably. Not sure about clothes. I'll go take a look in the bedrooms." He disappears back into the hall, and the sound of hinges creaking fills the silence as he opens the door to one of the bedrooms.

I walk into the dated kitchen, rummaging through various cupboards until I manage to find tea and mugs. There's a kettle already on the stove, so I fill it with water and ignite the burner. It's an old gas stove, so it takes a few tries to light, and while it starts to heat up, I drop tea bags into the mugs.

Atlas starts a fire in the fireplace across from the couch before sitting in a chair that looks about as comfortable as a rock and starts talking to Lex in a voice too quiet for me to hear.

I lean against the counter, closing my eyes as I listen to the kettle heating up. My thoughts drift to Gabriel, making my stomach sink. I can't help but feel as if we left him. Yes, we fled Washington because of the hunters, and Lex said this is only temporary, but we still left him. And with his psychotic ex and sire no less.

When Kade walks into the kitchen, I push away from the counter and approach him. "Any luck?"

He nods. "There isn't much, but it's enough to get out of the clothes we're in and wash them."

"Good." I press my lips together at the distant look in his usually bright silver eyes. "Kade…" My voice is soft, laced with concern. "Are you okay?" I lift my hand to his face, brushing my fingers against his cheek. I want to comfort him, take care of him. Because if I'm doing that, I won't have time to pay attention to the panic filling my veins, wrapping around my ribs, and squeezing my heart. When he exhales a shuddering breath, I realize his fangs are protruding from his gums.

"You need a drink." I move to step back and check the fridge for blood, but he wraps his fingers around my wrist, holding me in place.

"Slow down. It's all right, Calla."

"No. No, it's not. You—"

Kade kisses me. I try to pull back, to ask him what the hell he's doing, but he snakes his arm around my waist, hauling me against him and pinning me between him and the counter. His lips steal my breath, and eventually I can do nothing but succumb to the kiss. Closing my eyes, I relax against him and kiss him back. He's trying to distract me— probably himself too—and for a few moments, I'm going to let him.

When he pulls back, cupping my cheek and brushing his thumb over my skin, I meet his gaze and sigh. "I'm sorry about your sister," I tell him in a voice just barely above a whisper.

He kisses me once more, soft and quick. "Thanks."

The whistle of the kettle breaks us apart, and I walk to the stove and switch off the burner, pouring the water into each mug, before Kade and I carry them into the living room.

The four of us sit without speaking for a few minutes, sipping on tea and watching the flames dance in the fire- place, their soft crackling the only sound in the room.

I think I make it five minutes before I can't take the silence anymore. I set my mug on the oak coffee table and sit back in the black wingback chair. "What are we going to do now that your cover with the hunters is blown?"

Atlas looks to me. "Scott has been calling and texting me since we left Washington."

My chest feels tight at the mention of Brighton's father's name. "What did he say? Does he know I'm with you?"

"I'm not sure if he does," Atlas answers. "Likely not, as none of the hunters were people I recognized from the company, which leaves little chance they'd know who you are."

Lex sits up and takes a drink. "If Meredith is working

with the hunters, there's a chance she went back to them after her attack and told them there was a human with us, but that wouldn't mean that they'd figure out who."

"I haven't listened to Scott's voicemails—he left half a fucking dozen—but all his texts say is to call him back. A few empty threats here and there, but nothing seriously concerning at this point."

My eyes widen at his words. *Nothing seriously concerning?* I want to ask what would be considered seriously concerning to him, but I pick up my tea to sip instead. There are a lot of moving pieces, between Gabriel and Selene to Meredith and the hunters—they're all linked, and our best bet is to figure out what the hunters are planning now that they know Atlas, Kade, and Lex are vampires.

I wet my lips before saying, "So odds are the hunters have no idea who I am or my, um, association with you guys. That means there's a chance I can still—"

"Don't bother finishing that sentence," Atlas cuts in, snaring my gaze over the rim of his mug as he takes a drink of his tea. "You already know the answer."

I scowl. "In case you haven't noticed, you three are on the run. You're the vampires. The hunters have no reason to come after me."

"I'm sure they'll find one the minute they put it together that you're with us." Lex's jaw is set tight. If he grips that mug any tighter, it's going to shatter in his hands.

I reach over and pry it from his grip, setting it on the table in front of him. "We're not there yet," I point out. "Now's the time to use me while they're still in the dark. I can get in touch with Brighton and try to figure—"

"Enough."

My eyes snap back to Atlas and narrow. "Fine," I say through my teeth, "then what's your plan that's so clearly better than mine?"

A muscle feathers along his jaw as he holds my gaze, setting his mug down without a sound. "I need to speak with my contacts in New York. I actually put rational thought into my actions and consider the consequences before doing something."

I exhale a harsh breath, anger igniting in my chest as my pulse kicks up. "Oh, get off your high horse, Atlas." Defiance flares to life in me, and I continue, "You just don't want me to help, because god forbid someone else is the answer instead of you."

Kade sighs, exchanging a glance with Lex. "Here we go."

Atlas offers a bitter, humorless laugh. "You don't know a fucking thing."

I arch a brow, crossing my arms over my chest. "Please, enlighten me then."

"There are certain ways things need to be done," he says in a forced level tone. "Until you've lived for a century and understand that, I'm not going to waste my breath with this conversation."

That raises my hackles, and I snap, "You are so fucking arrogant."

"Okay, okay," Kade says, holding his hands up as if he's physically trying to contain the tension that hangs thick in the air. "Arguing about this isn't getting us any closer to a solution. Let's stop now before the two of you either start brawling or fucking in the middle of this sad excuse for a living room."

A mix of darkness and hunger fills Atlas's expression, making it harder to hold his gaze as my body betrays how I feel about Kade's latter concern. Heat swirls low in my belly at the thought of Atlas—*no*. I'm not going there.

I clear my throat, grabbing my empty mug off the coffee table and turning toward the kitchen. "I'll find something for dinner," I mutter, walking out of the room while I still have the will to fight the urge to take a swing at Atlas's infuriatingly attractive face. Fucking stupid supernatural beauty.

An hour later, we are sitting around a round dining table that is most definitely not big enough for four people. Lex and Kade are on either side of me and Atlas sits directly across from me. I managed to cook a beef teriyaki dish without burning the place down, so I'm calling it a win.

Lex and Kade devour their dishes, while I pick at mine, and Atlas leaves his untouched. Asshole. It may not be Gabriel's fancy cooking, but it's at least edible.

My expression must be more telling than I thought, because Atlas's lips twitch as he reaches for the glass of water in front of him.

"What?" I say through my teeth, gripping my fork so hard the metal bites into my fingers.

Atlas shakes his head and pushes his full dish away. "It's nothing personal. It actually smells quite good."

"But not good enough for you." I let go of my fork, letting it clammer against the dish before falling onto the table. "Because nothing is."

His eyes narrow ever so slightly. "Because," he says pointedly, "I need blood."

Oh. *Oh.*

Shit. The others survive off blood and food because they're turned vampires. Atlas can eat human food, but he gets no sustenance from it.

I shake my head, frowning. "I... There wasn't any in the fridge."

"I'm aware," he says. "It's fine."

I finish the water in my glass and am reaching for my knife before I even realize what I'm doing.

Lex catches my wrist. "Calla—"

"He needs blood," I say, holding my hand palm up. "You all do," I add, noticing Lex's fangs are showing.

"Do you know what you're doing?" Kade asks.

I spare him a short glance and nod. "I'm offering myself," I say, "to all of you." The words make me shiver, and my skin tingles where Lex's fingers are still wrapped around my wrist.

"Are you sure?" Lex asks.

"Are you going to kill me?" I ask the three vampires all looking at me as if I'm equal parts crazy and the answer to their prayers.

"Of course not," Kade says.

I nod again. "Then I'm sure. But maybe we shouldn't do this at the kitchen table?"

"Why not?" Atlas chimes in with a straight face. "You ate your dinner here."

I gape at him. I'm about to snap again, to revoke my offer to him specifically, when the unthinkable happens.

Atlas laughs.

*What the fuck?*

"Ease up, Calla. I'm only kidding."

I blink at him, utterly speechless. "I... Since when?"

The corner of his mouth tugs up, and he shrugs. "Perhaps you bring that out in me."

Heat fills my cheeks, and I want nothing more than to look away. Instead, I stand, setting the knife down. Lex follows my movement, keeping his gentle grip on my wrist, and we walk back into the living room, where I take a seat on the couch. Lex sits next to me on the right, and Kade drops onto the cushion on my left. Atlas walks into the room and stands behind the couch, leaning down and moving the hair away from my neck.

My heart pounds in my chest, threatening to break free of my ribcage, but I don't move. I take a deep breath and close my eyes as Kade and Lex each take one of my wrists while Atlas tilts my head back against the cushions. I press my lips together, whimpering softly when fangs sink into both of my wrists. Atlas's fingers dance along my skin, tracing over my collarbone as his lips graze the shell of my ear, and he whispers, "Breathe, Calla."

I let out a shaky breath, turning my cheek to expose my throat to him.

I don't expect him to hesitate. I don't expect his lips to brush my neck, to kiss my skin. His hand slides against my cheek, cradling my head, and then his fangs finally sink into my neck. My whimper from before is replaced by a breathy moan. The sensation of blood being pulled from me in three different directions leaves me feeling light and warm, and has my core throbbing almost in time with my racing pulse.

The vampires on either side of me slide their hands up my thighs, getting dangerously close to the heat between them, and I bite my lip against the pleasure flooding through me. Can I blame it on the venom coursing through my veins? Because I'm definitely going to.

Kade and Lex pull back, sealing the wounds on my wrists as Atlas continues drinking. A moment later, he finishes, dragging his tongue along my neck slowly as his thumb glides back and forth over my skin. His hand against my cheek keeps my head from lolling to the side, and I fight to pry my eyes open despite wanting to keep them shut. To live in this haze of pleasure and warmth and forget about all the problems we're facing outside of this safe house.

"Calla." Kade pats my knee. "Wakey, wakey. You need to eat something."

"No," I groan, trying to wave him off, "I need to sleep."

"Open your eyes." Atlas's command latches onto me, and my eyes open in an instant. "Good. Now, Kade is going to go get your dinner and bring it in here, and you're going to eat it."

"Hmm... I want grilled cheese."

Lex laughs. "I mean, it's the least we can do. We did just have *her* for dinner." He glances at Atlas. "Give the girl what she wants."

Atlas's fingers slip away from my cheek, and he and Kade walk back to the kitchen while Lex pulls me into his lap, curling his arm around my waist. His fingers trail under my shirt, skimming the skin below my belly button, and my breath hitches. He chuckles softly but doesn't move his fingers any lower, so I relax against him.

After I've devoured two grilled cheese sandwiches, I'm feeling steady enough on my feet to put some distance between myself and any furniture—or vampires—to hold me up. I excuse myself and go in search of the washroom, which I find at the end of the hall. It's nothing special, nothing like what I'd gotten used to at the guy's place. In fact, it's reminiscent of the bathroom in my apartment, and I find myself smiling at the memory. It's strange how long ago that part of my life feels now, when really, it was only just over a month ago. So much has happened these past weeks, it's hard to think of what my life was like before this. Before *them*.

After a lukewarm shower—because this place evidently doesn't have a very strong water heater—I dress in a T-shirt I found in one of the bedroom dressers and pop my head back into the living room to say goodnight.

They don't try to stop me or join me, and while part of me is a little disappointed by that, I'm mostly grateful for the space.

The bedroom I pick has light yellow walls and a four-poster dark wood bed with white sheets. Pulling back the heavy comforter, the faint smell of fabric softener tickles my nose, and I crawl under the sheets, the mattress creaking under me. There's a small table beside the bed with a lamp that's probably older than I am, casting the small room in a soft golden glow.

With a deep breath, I roll over and flick the light out before settling onto my back. I stare at the ceiling, my eyes fluttering shut to the sound of muffled conversation from the living room. Their presence brings me comfort enough to snuggle into this strange bed and pretend I'm somewhere else.

In minutes, sleep drags me under, and I go willingly.

⁂

When my eyes open, ice fills my veins, and I shoot upright, gasping for air that isn't there. My eyes whip around the elegant space, and my stomach sinks. *I can't be back here.* The room comes more into focus, and I shake my head. "No…" I scramble off the bed and rush toward the window, my head spinning when all I can see outside is darkness. I whirl around, walking past the blazing fireplace and toward the door, but just like last time, before I can reach for the handle, the door opens. I jump back, gritting my teeth as I wait for Selene to glide in and taunt me once again.

Except, it isn't Selene.

I suck in a breath, hot tears pricking my eyes. "Gabriel?"

He steps into the room, closing the door behind him, and smiles at me. "Hello, angel."

I have no idea what's happening right now, but I throw my arms around his neck, clinging to him with every ounce of strength I have. Granted, that isn't much right now.

Gabriel circles his arms around my waist, holding me against him, and buries his face in the crook of my neck. "I don't know how much time we have," he murmurs.

I close my eyes, inhaling deeply, melting into him. "What do you mean? Isn't this a dream?"

"Calla." His voice isn't unkind, but it has lost its dreamlike warmth.

I pull back enough to look at his face, to run my fingers through his thick copper hair, to gaze into his soft, silver eyes. "What is it?" My brows knit in confusion. "Is… is this *real?*"

He nods. "It's a dream in the sense that you're asleep wherever you are, but I am very much awake."

I shake my head. "I don't understand."

Gabriel offers a small laugh. "I don't either. Not fully. But we don't have time to question it when we don't know if or when it'll end."

I pull in a sharp breath. "The hunters. Gabriel—"

"I know, angel." He frowns. "Selene made a deal with Scott. She traded the names of at least a dozen powerful vampires in the city in exchange for her own protection."

My mouth drops open. "Selene told the hunters where we live. They ambushed the house, and we had to run."

His jaw clenches as the color drains from his face. "Is—"

"Everyone is fine," I rush to tell him. "But, um… Kade. His sister is alive. She's a vampire, and I think she's working with the hunters like Selene is."

His eyes widen. "That's not good. How is he?"

Sighing, I say, "He's putting on a strong face, but I don't think he's okay." I can't imagine how he could be.

Gabriel nods. "Right. Of course he isn't."

I chew my bottom lip, my eyes flicking between his. "How are *you?*"

He smiles sadly.

"Oh, Gabriel." I reach for him again, sliding my hands up his chest. "I wish you were here."

He cups my cheek. "I wish for that too."

I turn my face and press my lips against his palm. "The whole reason you went to Selene was because of her threat against me. The solution to that was to kill her, which we were holding off on doing because we wanted to know more about her relationship with the hunters. Since she outed the guys to the hunters, I don't see why her relationship to them matters much now."

"I didn't know about that until you told me," he says gently.

I scowl. "Of course she kept it from you. Is she still playing the angle that she missed you and wants to be with you?"

He tilts his head, regarding me thoughtfully. "It doesn't matter, angel. I didn't miss her, nor do I want to be with her. Now that I know what she's done, you're absolutely right. There's no sense in keeping her alive."

"Good, so—"

He leans in, pressing his forehead against mine. "But there's nothing you or I can do about that right now. I'm here with her, unable to strike her down myself, and you are somewhere I imagine is far enough away to keep you safe. So how about we just enjoy each other's company while we have it and until we can be together for real?"

The pressure in my chest expands, sending a burst of warmth between my legs, making me throb with desire.

"Are you asking me for dream sex?" I ask, not even attempting to hide my amusement.

Gabriel grins at me. "I very much am, yes."

My nose grazes his, and I brush my lips along his bottom one, kissing him slowly, teasingly. He drops his hands to my hips and spins us around, pinning me against the door before his lips claim mine, taking control of the kiss in a single breath. His tongue glides along my lips, and I part them, letting him in and moaning into his mouth when he presses his lower half against me, igniting a delicious friction between my thighs. He knows where to apply pressure to send a bolt of electricity straight to my clit, and I gasp against his lips.

I break away to moan his name, my nipples stiffening against the T-shirt I fell asleep in. It's currently riding up my thighs, held in place by Gabriel's fingers digging into my hips.

"I want nothing more than to take my time tasting every bit of your exquisite body, but I fear our time will run out too quickly."

I don't think I can handle slow tonight. "Please," I breathe, "I need you inside me."

He picks me up easily, and I hang onto his shoulders as he turns us around and walks to the bed, laying me down before tugging his shirt off, dropping it onto the floor. He does the same with his pants and boxers, leaving him naked where he stands at the end of the bed.

I'm propped up on my elbows, watching his every move. I grab the hem of my shirt, pulling it over my head and tossing it to the side, letting Gabriel see me as I'm seeing him— completely bare.

He crawls over me, pressing his lips just above my belly button, his tongue swirling against my skin and kicking my pulse up. He drags his lips up my stomach, peppering soft kisses along the way, making goosebumps rise on my skin as I press my lips together. My core throbs, and almost as if he senses my need, he presses his knee there, and I let out a breathy moan, pushing my fingers through his hair. His lips close around my nipple, and heat shoots right to my clit, making it overly sensitive. My back arches, pushing my breast into his mouth, where his tongue swirls around my nipple, alternating between sucking and licking. Then he moves to the other side, and repeats his ministrations, leaving me panting beneath him.

"Gabriel," I say, gripping his hair between my fingers with one hand and reaching for his cock with the other. I can feel the wetness already gathering between my legs, and he hasn't even touched me there yet. But I need him to. Now.

I wrap my fingers around his thick length, guiding him to my entrance. I drag the blunt head of his cock along my folds, licking the dryness from my lips before kissing him deeply. I whimper against his mouth when he takes hold of his cock and presses it against my clit before dipping inside of me slowly. I lift my hips, pushing him in deeper, and he groans against my lips. We find a delicious rhythm in no time, and Gabriel alternates between kissing my lips and sucking on the sensitive skin below my ear as he rolls his hips and thrusts into me, slow and deep, then hard and fast until I'm seeing fucking stars.

"Gabriel," I pant, digging my heels into his ass to push him even deeper.

"I know," he says against my skin as his thrusts become more frantic. "Come for me, angel."

His words trigger my release, and my pussy clenches around him, milking his cock as he continues to thrust into me, the sound of his grunts mixing with my moans as he climaxes next, filling me with his release.

Once the aftershocks of my orgasm fade, Gabriel kisses the corner of my mouth and pulls out of me, dropping onto the bed beside me and pulling me against him. I close my eyes, my cheek pressed against his chest as his heart returns to a steady beat.

"Can we stay here?" I murmur with a yawn.

He brushes my hair away from my face, tucking it behind my ear before dropping a kiss to my forehead. "I wish we could. But unfortunately, you need to wake up."

My bubble of warmth and happiness pops, and I frown up at him. "But we haven't been here that long."

He offers me a soft smile. "It's morning."

I blink at him, confusion filling me. "That much time has passed?" Disbelief fills my tone.

He nods. "I'm sorry. I'll see you soon, angel, and we'll figure everything out. I promise."

I want to say more, to hold him longer, but before I can open my mouth to speak, his face starts to fade. Everything around me goes dark, stealing the scene from me slowly and then all at once.

## 3

## KADE

I'm up before the others, having slept on the couch instead of trying to squeeze into the second bedroom with Atlas and Lex. I considered slipping into Calla's room, but something told me she needed space from us. A bed to herself for the night was the least we could give her.

I didn't sleep much anyway. Not with the flashes of Meredith's face twisted in bitter anger and the sight of her razor-sharp fangs bared at me playing on a vicious loop every time I closed my eyes.

After an all too short workout outside, I take a quick, scorching shower and pull the only clothing I have out of the dryer.

The shitty coffee maker in the kitchen is my next stop after getting dressed. It's a far cry from the machine we had installed in our kitchen, but desperate times and whatnot.

I lean against the counter, glancing around the small, outdated room in the dim morning light just barely starting to filter through the window over the sink. I pull out my phone to check for any communications from Marcel while the machine gurgles softly behind me, filling the space with a warm, rich aroma that calls to me almost as strongly as the scent of blood. Almost.

With a cup of coffee in hand, I walk back to my makeshift couch bed, my steps silent across the peel and stick linoleum in the kitchen to the hardwood in the living room. There's a bit of a chill in the air, and instead of fighting with the thermostat, I strike a match across the brick fireplace and start a fire inside. The flames fill the room with a soft glow and warmth as I lounge on the couch, sipping my coffee. It's almost peaceful—you know, if I could ignore the reason we're here.

Lex rises next, his white hair an absolute mess, which he clearly couldn't give two shits about. He doesn't acknowledge my presence until he has a cup of coffee in his hand. He sits in one of the chairs across from me, glancing into the flames.

"You sleep?" he asks in a deep, tired voice.

"Not much. You?"

He grumbles his agreement.

Atlas's voice reaches me, though he's still in the other room. Sounds like he's on the phone with one of Marcel's guys, arranging for a blood delivery. Good man. As much as I'd prefer Calla's blood over the bagged stuff, we can't all feed from her over and over.

He joins us after ending the call, foregoing the coffee, and drops into the chair next to Lex.

I set my empty mug on the coffee table and sigh. Before I can say anything, Calla's bedroom door creaks open. She makes a stop in the bathroom before padding out to the living room, glancing between each of us, and plops onto the opposite end of the couch.

"Morning," she murmurs, sleep still clinging to her soft voice.

I want to pull her to me, lay her across my lap, and coax her back to sleep. Like the rest of us, she looks exhausted.

She bites her lip, glancing at her lap as her pulse ticks faster.

"What is it?" Lex asks before I can.

"I… had a dream last night. Or, I think it was a dream. I don't know." She looks up again and pushes her fingers through her dark brown hair, pulling it up and tying it into a knot on the top of her head.

"You don't know?" Atlas questions, arching a brow at her.

"I think it was real somehow. I saw Gabriel. I mean, he was with me."

My brows inch up my forehead, and I look from her to the guys to see similar reactions on their faces. We're all confused as fuck. Dreamwalking isn't a vampiric ability that I'm aware of. I steal a glance at Atlas; if any of us would know about it, he would. But he appears as lost as I am by this revelation.

"It could be part of the bond," Lex offers. "We can't say we know everything about the oath, especially when there was a witch involved, right? Maybe Gabriel was able to use his connection to you to reach you while unconscious."

"I was asleep," she says, "but Gabriel was awake."

"Interesting," Lex muses, sipping his coffee. "Perhaps the rest of us should test it out. See if we can all appear in your dream at the same time."

"I've never heard of this," Atlas comments mildly. "It doesn't seem too far outside the realm of possibility, though."

"I wonder if that witch Tessa, the one Selene sent to heal me, could tell us about it," Calla muses aloud. "Do you think we could track her down? I mean, after we get Gabriel back, deal with the hunters, save the world, and all that."

"Funny," I mutter, shaking my head. I understand her curiosity—hell, I'd like to know more about this dreamwalking Gabriel was able to do—but I'd rather not bring a witch into the mix.

"It's something to consider," she says, "and Tessa seemed pretty cool."

"For a witch," Lex grumbles under his breath, and my lips almost curl into a grin.

"What exactly happened in this dream? What did Gabriel say to you?" I ask, my chest feeling oddly tight. Every minute Gabriel is away from us, the pit of worry in my gut grows heavier. There's a sharp pain there too, an ugly flare of jealousy that Calla got to see him, even if only in a dream. We need to get him back for real and take out the psycho blond who has her claws in him.

None of us miss the tinge of pink in Calla's cheeks as she presses her lips together.

"He, uh…" She clears her throat, shaking her head as if to clear it and focus, then starts again. "Selene sold us out. Whatever deal she made with Scott to cover her own ass, she used us to fulfill her end and told the hunters you three are vampires and where to find you."

I grip the armrest of the couch so tight, my fingers tear into the leather. My fangs threaten to slice through my gums as I bite back a growl. Lex looks about five seconds away from exploding with anger, and Atlas is scarily still, his jaw sharp enough to cut glass.

"We're getting him back," I snarl, feeling Calla shift closer to me. She wraps her arm around mine, leaning into me. Glancing down, I blink at her in surprise. I'm not used to someone moving closer when I'm pissed off.

"We will," Lex assures me with a stiff nod.

"No more waiting. We know what Selene is up to with the hunters now—selling us out." Bitterness laces my tone, and the urge to get my fingers around her neck and squeeze until her eyes bulge out of her face is overwhelming.

"I've been thinking about it," Calla says. "I think she

figured with us out of the way, Gabriel would be more inclined to stay with her. He'd have no one else."

"That bitch is dead," Lex growls.

"We need to be careful," Atlas chimes in, his posture unnaturally straight. "Considering we're essentially fugitives, and there are hunters all over the place, it could get tricky to return to Washington."

"Fuck that," Lex snaps, his eyes wild—more so than normal—and blazing with anger.

"Lex," Atlas warns, shooting him a dark look. "Take a breath. We'll get him back and deal with Selene, but we need to be smart about how we proceed."

Calla sighs, getting off the couch and walking into the kitchen. A minute later, she returns, cradling a steaming cup of coffee. "Not to sound selfish or anything, but I still have school. The term is almost over, but unless you see us resolving this whole hunter issue over the summer break, I'll need to figure out what I'm doing come the fall. I understand this isn't any of your main concerns, but school is quite literally the only normal thing I have left in my life, so yeah, I'm worried about it."

I stare at her, my gums throbbing as I clench my jaw. I want to be sympathetic and understanding of her concerns, but I can't find the will to give a shit about her going to school. We have much bigger problems to face at the moment—including my sister who I believed to be dead for over a century.

Standing, I walk around the couch and leave the room before I say something that'll only upset her. I find myself in the bedroom the guys slept in, leaning against the wall and looking out the window to the side of the property where the sun is rising.

I hear Lex come in and close the door before he speaks, but I don't turn around.

"Kade—"

"Don't," I cut him off.

He sighs, walking closer. "Talk to me, brother."

With a groan, I turn to face him, leaning against the windowsill. "I didn't want to be a dick, so I removed myself from the situation where I was very close to becoming one."

His lips twitch.

"Don't fucking grin at that."

He doesn't try to hide it. "Come on, Kade. You should be celebrating. I think this is real growth for you."

I glare at him. "Prick."

Lex comes closer, stopping once he's close enough to grab ahold of my shoulders. "I know this is stressful for you. Different from how it's affecting the rest of us. I can only imagine what's going through your head right now, but you're not alone." His fingers dig into my shoulders, massaging them until the tension is forced out.

I hold his gaze and nod.

His hands glide off my shoulders, moving down my bare arms, and when his fingers go to work on my belt, my lips curl into a faint grin. "What are you doing?"

He gets the buckle undone and pops the button on my pants. "I'm going to help work out some of that stress." He shoots me a wink, and I roll my eyes but make no move to stop him. Because as pissed as I am, my cock is already hard, twitching and aching to be touched.

Lex pulls my zipper down slowly, the sound echoing through the room as my heart rate kicks up. He wastes no time sliding his fingers into my boxers and pulling my cock out. He bends slightly, tugging my pants down to just above my knees, then straightens, looking me in the eyes.

I suck in a sharp breath through my teeth and grip the windowsill on either side of me as he wraps his fingers around my thick length and starts moving his hand up and down. I close my eyes, and my head falls back against the window with a thud. It could shatter the glass for all I care, so long as Lex keeps his hand on my dick.

A groan rips through me when he applies pressure, twisting his grip as he pumps and using his free hand to massage my balls. He pauses at the blunt tip of my cock for a moment, rubbing his thumb through the moisture gathering there until I growl at him to keep moving, and he returns to the torturous rhythm of pumping.

My chest rises and falls fast as Lex increases both his pressure and pace, and I grab his shoulder to steady myself. "Don't fucking stop," I bark out, and he chuckles deeply. The sound goes straight to my cock, and everything tightens. I let out a deep grunt, and my release spurts out over his hand.

After we've cleaned up, I pull my pants up and buckle my belt.

"You good?" Lex checks as we head toward the bedroom door.

"Better." I nod at him. "Thanks."

He offers another wink. "Anytime. And I fully expect you to return the favor next time." It's not like we haven't done this before, though it has been a while. Over the years, we've all been together in one way or another. Sometimes one-on-one, other times all together. When you know someone for over a century and build such a unique and strong bond, societal norms really don't matter. How you feel about another person—or *people*, in our case—is far more important.

I laugh, opening the door and stepping into the hallway. "Of course you do."

Back in the living room, we find Atlas and Calla bickering about needing to get back to Washington unnoticed, to get Gabriel out of Selene's clutches before any more damage can be done.

Calla leans against the back of the couch, crossing her arms over her chest. "We know where they are, granted Selene didn't move after throwing you guys under the bus with the hunters, but I don't see why she'd do that. And in my dream, we were in the same penthouse, which could also mean they're still there."

"We'll get him back," Lex assures her, perching on the armrest next to her. "Then we'll figure out what to do about the hunters."

Atlas says nothing, just rubs his hand along his jaw as he glances out the front window.

"The way I see it," Calla says, "we have two choices. Try to work with the hunters by showing them you're not a danger to the humans… or take them out." She glances between us, settling her determined gaze on Atlas. "Are you prepared to declare war?"

His jaw clenches. "That's not my call."

Her brows pinch together as she blinks at him. "Isn't it?"

"Atlas is one of a group of born vampires. His parents basically run the vampire world. He'll need to consult with them."

She catches her bottom lip between her teeth and nods. "And where are they?"

"The big apple," Lex chimes in with a faint grin despite the serious topic of conversation.

Her eyes widen and the beat of her heart shifts, becoming more uneven, as if the thought of the city she grew up leaves her uneasy. "Great," she finally says, "let's get going."

"We're not going to New York," Atlas says.

"Then what are we going to do?" Her voice is strained, and my eyes follow her hand as she seemingly reaches for the dagger at her thigh without conscious thought.

"Take a breath," Lex suggests, his gaze tracking her movement as well. "This shit isn't something we're going to figure out in a matter of an hour."

"He's right," Atlas confirms, looking rather pleased by her instinctive reach for the weapon he gave her.

She scowls, frowning when her phone chimes beside her. The three of us watch her pick it up and read the notification.

"What is it?" Lex asks.

Calla glances up, and her deep brown eyes flit between us as she realizes we're all staring at her. "Relax, guys. It's just Brighton." She taps away on the screen for a few seconds, then sets her phone face down on the coffee table. "Our usual brunch spot is closed on Monday for some private event, so we have to go somewhere else."

"You're not going anywhere near her," Atlas says in a dangerously calm voice.

She's quick to turn a glare on him. "Not going would be worse," she points out. "I've barely spoken to her since being taken by Selene, and she probably already thinks things are weird considering I'm still not back to school." She crosses her arms. "I have to go. I need to see her, and she needs to see that I'm fine, otherwise she's going to start asking questions we don't want."

I purse my lips, looking to Atlas, though he's still staring at her. She's not wrong. The last thing we need is for Brighton to express concern over her BFF to that stab-happy father of hers and mention the sexy group of guys Calla was hanging with at the St. Patrick's Day party last month.

"I have an idea," I offer. "Let's say we let her go. We can pick the location and have our team surround it. Keep eyes on her at all times."

She arches a brow at me. "Because that's not creepy or anything."

"You want to go or not?" I warn. "I'm trying to help you here."

"This is ridiculous," she complains. "Brighton, for one, isn't a hunter. She doesn't even know about them." She shakes her head. "We've had this conversation before and it hasn't changed."

I nod slowly. "If you want to see her, you'll agree to the terms I've laid out."

Lex grumbles in agreement, and Atlas lets a heavy silence hang in the air for several moments before he agrees as well.

She rolls her eyes. "Fine. If that's what it takes."

## CALLA

I could easily make a list of things I'd rather do than spend Monday morning stuck in a car with Atlas, but perhaps I should be grateful he decided to drive me back to Washington to have brunch with Brighton. That being said, I hadn't considered that would mean being locked in the car with him for over three hours. I'd hoped Kade or Lex—or both, honestly—would join us, but they were still asleep when we left the safe house.

Atlas has his phone connected to the sound system, and I'm surprised at how much I don't hate his taste in music. I was expecting hardcore rock or angsty screamo. So when Halsey's *Young God* comes on, I turn my shocked expression to him.

"Why are you staring at me?" he asks after a moment without taking his eyes off the road.

"Uh, no reason. I just… didn't peg you for a Halsey fan," I comment mildly.

"What *did* you peg me for, Calla?" There's a hint of curiosity in his deep voice that has my lips twitching.

"Hmm, you really don't want me to answer that."

He offers a short laugh. "Why? Because I'll be tempted to pull over and show you just how wrong you are about me?"

Boldness grips me, and I say, "Hate to break it to you, but that's not the threat you think it is."

He grips the steering wheel tighter, his jaw working. "And why is that? Because it's exactly what you want?"

*Absolutely fucking right it is.* We've been playing this deadly game of cat and mouse for over a month now. Something needs to happen before one of us explodes.

I chew my lower lip, pressing my thighs together as heat gathers between them. Swallowing past the sudden dryness in my throat, I say, "Doesn't matter, because you won't do it."

"No?" he challenges.

"You're not going to fuck me in the back seat of your car." The doubt is clear in my voice despite how it shakes. Because as sure as I am that he won't do it, there's a depraved part of me that longs for him to do just that. To show me who he truly is—no holding back. The fear, the not knowing what he's fully capable of, it's dangerously exciting.

Atlas shoots me a dark look that steals my breath. "Who said anything about the back seat?" He shakes his head, returning his gaze to the road as his lips curl into a smirk. "I'd fuck you up here with your back against the steering wheel and let everyone driving by see how easily I can make you scream for me."

My heart slams against my chest, and I tear my eyes away from him, the car suddenly suffocating. I feel Atlas everywhere. As hard as I try to shove him out of my head, it's useless.

"Nothing to say now, huh?" he taunts, gripping the wheel so hard his knuckles are white.

"Pull over," I say, nearly breathless. I need a minute without the movement of this car; I need air.

"You really—"

"Atlas, so help me, *pull over.*"

In the space of a heartbeat, he jerks the wheel to the side, guiding the car off the interstate. Gravel crunches under the tires and kicks up dust, and I have my seat belt off, reaching for the door before Atlas even puts the car in park.

The second the lock clicks open, I all but throw myself outside, slamming the door shut before walking toward the thick line of pine trees that run along the freeway. I make it into the damp forest, the sounds of the cars speeding down the interstate fading into the background as I slowly find my center again.

I hug my arms around myself, attempting to suck in deep breaths of fresh, spring air, but when Atlas appears in front of me, I choke on the air in my throat and come to an abrupt stop.

"What the fuck is the matter with you?" His eyes are narrowed and filled with irritation. "Get back in the car."

"With *me?*" I force out in a sharp tone, taking a healthy step back. "Says the guy who was just talking about fucking me for any passerby to watch."

His hands curl into fists at his sides as his blazing silver gaze dances across my face. He takes a step closer. Then another. One more step, and we're so close the tops of his shoes are almost touching my Docs. Atlas cocks his head to the side, and I hold my breath as he studies me. "That's not why you're angry," he finally says.

I arch a brow at him. "Wh—"

"You're upset because you *want* it."

My mouth drops open, and I grasp for the words to refute his accusation, but nothing forms. Fucking hell. I hate him. More than that, I hate that he's right. The thought of people watching him claim me… My chest flushes, and I desperately want to look away so he can't see the heat in my cheeks.

He chuckles deeply, and before I know what's happening,

my fist is swinging toward his face, toward the smug smirk plastered across his lips.

It doesn't connect. *Of course* it doesn't. Instead, Atlas catches my fist in his hand and grips it tightly, pushing me back until I collide with the thick trunk of a tree, its bark rough against my thin windbreaker.

I pull my fist back, and he lets it go. In the time it takes me to blink, he cages me against the tree, his hands braced on either side of my head. My eyes widen at his dark expression, at the sharpness of his jaw. But instead of ducking under his arm and attempting to put distance between us, I press my hands to his hard chest.

"What are you doing?" he growls.

I hold his gaze, the pressure in my chest building. "What are *you* doing?"

He exhales harshly, leaning down so his lips are level with my ear, which presses him so close, my hands are effectively trapped between his chest and mine. "I haven't quite decided yet." His words trigger a shiver to shoot down my spine, and I turn my face away.

In hindsight, that probably wasn't the best move, considering it bares my neck to him.

Atlas wraps his fingers around my throat and presses his thumb against my jaw, forcing my gaze back to him. "I have you all alone out here." He lowers his voice. "There is no one to stop me from doing whatever I want to you." He flicks his tongue over his bottom lip, and I catch sight of his fangs. He chuckles darkly when I suck in a breath. "And you'd let me, wouldn't you?" The fire in his eyes sends heat straight to my core, making my entire body flush under his scrutiny, though he isn't glamouring me.

"You're trying to scare me," I force out in a level tone, shaking my head. "I'm not going anywhere."

The corner of his mouth curls up slowly. "I wouldn't let you if you tried."

My heart is beating so hard I can feel it in my throat. "So do it then," I taunt despite my racing pulse.

He drops his hands to my hips, where his fingers dig into my skin, and though there's a layer of clothing between his skin and mine, heat courses through me. "What, you're not going to fight me anymore?"

I pause, the heat between my legs throbbing with need. "Not today."

A faint growl rumbles in his chest, and he dips his head, sealing his lips over mine in a fiery kiss that swallows my entire world so there's nothing left but him.

My fingers end up in his stupidly soft hair as his trail under my jacket and shirt, teasing upward toward my bra. Our lips battle for control, neither willing to succumb to the other. When his fang slices my lip, spilling my blood into his mouth, his body tenses against mine, the hardness between his legs pressing where I crave him most.

I can't stop the moan that escapes my lips, muffled by his mouth on mine. He leans back, his fangs fully extended and my blood staining his lips. Perhaps the sight should frighten or disturb me. Instead, it only makes me ache for him.

"Calla," he warns, seeing something in my gaze.

I press my lips together, then offer him a faint smile. "How long are you going to make me wait, Atlas?"

He licks my blood from his lips. "Forgive me," he says in a dry tone, "for showing some restraint so as not to fuck you against a tree. How rude of me."

I roll my eyes. "Don't pretend to be a gentleman," I retort. "You were ready to take me in the front seat of your car on the side of the interstate five minutes ago." I palm the bulge in his pants. "Hmm. It certainly feels like you're ready now."

Atlas hisses, grabbing my wrist, but doesn't pull it away.

Instead, he captures my lips again, kissing me until my head spins, and loosens his grip on my wrist. I take that as an invitation to keep palming him through his pants, and am quickly rewarded with a deep groan from him. One of his hands slides back up my shirt while the other presses flat against my stomach, then glides under the waistband of my leggings. The moment his fingers brush my folds, electricity crackles through me, and I gasp against his lips.

"Fucking hell," he says against my lips, his voice ragged. "You're practically dripping for me already."

Before I can beg for his fingers, he plunges two inside me, dragging his lips away from my mouth and along my jaw. My hips jerk forward, but he shoves me back against the tree.

"I control this," he says, circling my clit with his thumb as his fingers continue moving, massaging the walls of my pussy.

I pull my bottom lip between my teeth to keep from snapping at him. I won't risk him stopping the movement of his fingers. Fuck, if he needs to be in control, so be it. I'll gladly give it up so long as he doesn't stop.

He undoes my bra, and I've never been so grateful for front clasp bras as when he starts palming my breast, rolling the nipple between his fingers until my breath hitches.

"Yes," I moan.

He picks up the pace of his thrusting fingers and switches to my other breast. My head falls against the tree, my back arching as I push my breast into his skilled hand. When he adds pressure to the thumb against my clit and starts curling his fingers inside me, I suck in a shallow breath, my heart rate kicking up and my knees starting to shake.

"Calla."

My name on his lips makes my pussy clench around his fingers, shooting another wave of pleasure through me.

His voice is low, thick with arousal when he says, "Are you going to come?"

A grin tugs at my lips as tension continues to build between my legs. "You'll feel pretty inadequate if I don't, now won't you?"

"Go ahead," he taunts, "try not to."

There's a challenge in his gaze that I'm tempted to accept, but when his fingers brush a particularly sensitive spot deep inside me, everything tightens seconds before an orgasm rips through me, stealing the breath from my lungs with a deep, loud moan and making my knees buckle.

Atlas catches me around the waist, holding me up, and chuckles. "Valiant effort," he remarks dryly.

I grip the front of his T-shirt, leaning into him as I catch my breath. "Couldn't have you moping the rest of the way to Washington."

He leans in, brushing his lips across mine in a whisper of a kiss. "Stop talking." He presses closer, curling his fingers into the waistband of my leggings, and tugs them down to my knees. "I'm nowhere near done with you, and we're running out of time if you actually wish to make it to Washington."

My stomach clenches with a warm mixture of nerves and excitement, and I reach for him, fumbling with his pants until I get the front open. Before I can slide my fingers past the band of his Calvin Klein boxers, he catches my wrists, and I look up at him, instantly caught in his liquid silver gaze.

"I won't be gentle," he warns.

"I don't care," I breathe.

His nostrils flare, and he shakes his head. "I'm not sure if you're the worst thing for me..." His voice drops. "Or the only thing I need."

"Atlas," I whisper, and he closes his eyes, freeing my

wrists. I lift my hands to his face, my fingers grazing his cheeks and the dark stubble along his jaw. I lean up on my tip toes, ignoring the way the bark catches on my windbreaker as I press my lips against his.

He kisses me back, slow and soft at first, but it quickly turns to something far more frantic. We can't get enough of each other. And when I feel the blunt head of his cock teasing my entrance, my pulse races, and I tug him harder against me. He grips my hip with one hand and his cock with the other. Dragging the tip along the length of my slit, he drives me crazy, his lips moving against mine, tasting me—claiming me. When his tongue darts out, flicking along my lips, I part them, letting him in, and gasp into his mouth as he presses his cock against my clit. My hips jerk against him, and he deepens the kiss, grazing his tongue along mine.

Without warning, he fills my pussy with his cock, stretching me and knocking the air out of my lungs. His previous ministrations left me wet enough for him to glide in with one smooth, deep thrust of his hips.

My hands drop to his shoulders, and I hang on, digging my fingers in as I try to adjust to his size. He holds still inside of me, breaking the kiss, and I suck in a breath, my chest rising and falling quickly.

"Relax," he says gruffly, "you're gripping my cock like a vise."

I exhale on a short, breathy laugh. "A little warning next time would be nice."

He leans in, pressing his lips against my cheek. "I did warn you," he murmurs.

*I won't be gentle.*

Well, fuck me.

I turn my face and capture his lips again, circling my hips as much as I can trapped between Atlas and the tree. The sound he makes against my lips is a delicious mix between a growl and a groan, and it shoots heat to my core.

His lips move to my neck, kissing and sucking there as he pulls out slowly before slamming back into me. He reaches between us to tease my clit with his fingers as he continues his vicious rhythm of hard and deep thrusts.

My head falls back against the tree, and I close my eyes, biting my lip as pleasure floods through me in waves, pushing me closer to the edge.

"Open your eyes," he orders, and I obey without a second of hesitation. "If only you always listened so attentively." He smirks, then adds, "Keep them on me. I want to see your face when you come on my cock."

My cheeks fill with heat, but I hold his gaze as he continues his wicked pace, slowing for a few thrusts before slamming into me so fast my head spins. His fingers circle my clit hard and fast until I'm panting, practically writhing against him.

"Atlas," I breathe, the walls of my pussy clenching around him as the pressure builds to an almost unbearable level.

"You want to come?" he says in my ear, making the hair on the back of my neck stand straight, and slows his pace again, pulling me back from the edge.

I grit my teeth and nod quickly.

He rolls his hips, hitting a new spot, and nips my earlobe. "Say it. Tell me how much you need it."

"Asshole," I grumble.

He holds is cock still inside me and moves his fingers away from my clit, leaning back to look into my eyes and smirk at me. "Try again."

I lick the dryness from my lips and hold his glimmering gaze. "I need you," I force the words out, "to make me come."

He wraps his fingers around my throat, holding me against the tree, and drives his cock into me at an unrelenting pace. With skilled, perfectly timed thrusts, he launches me over the edge, making my body ignite with such a powerful orgasm, my world narrows. Everything clenches, and I cry out my release, gasping his name. I cling to him to stay upright as his thrusts become faster and harder until he grunts deeply, spilling his own release into me.

Atlas claims my mouth as I ride the aftershocks of my orgasm. He pulls back, giving me a moment to catch my breath, and glides out of me. Tucking himself into his pants, he does them up before tugging my leggings back up.

"Will you get back in the car now?"

I consider it for a moment, tilting my head to the side. "Maybe."

His eyes narrow ever so slightly. "You truly enjoy testing me, don't you?"

I shrug. "Maybe."

He shakes his head and places his hand against the small of my back, guiding me the way we came.

Once we're back in the car, I cross my legs, pressing my lips together at the delicious ache between my thighs. "Hmm, you know, I thought about moaning Kade's name just to mess with you, but even I can admit to being too scared of your response to go through with it."

Atlas pulls back onto the interstate, and a muscle feathers along his jaw before his lips twitch. "Wise choice."

❧

It's mid-afternoon when we reach Washington. I texted Brighton from the car that I'd be a little late, and when we pull up outside the Tryst café, my stomach is more filled with nerves than I was expecting.

"Calla." Atlas's uncharacteristically soft voice snares my

attention, and I turn toward him. "You don't have to do this. Say the word, and I'll handle it."

I smile. "I can't do much about our current… situation, but I can do this." I pull in an uneven breath. "I just need a minute."

"Take as many as you need."

"Can you glamour me not to be so freaking nervous?" I ask with a laugh to show him I'm only kidding; the thought of being glamoured still freaks me out.

"I could," he says, "but I don't think I need to."

His confidence in me is weirdly empowering. So much so, I square my shoulders, take a deep breath, and reach for the door handle.

"We'll have eyes on you at all times. Anything feels off, you get up and walk to the door. Our team will keep you safe."

I glance at him over my shoulder. "And where will you be?"

A dangerous glint fills his eyes. "I'm going to get Gabriel."

I turn back to face him completely, my pulse jackhammering. "What? No. I want to go with you."

He laughs, but it holds little humor. "Too bad. You already have plans."

"Atlas." I glare at him.

"Go on." He nods toward the café. "Out of my car."

I shake my head, knowing full well there's no sense arguing with him. I climb out of the Escalade and slam the door, just in case my death glare wasn't enough to show him that I'm pissed.

He pulls away from the curb, leaving me staring after him until the vehicle disappears around the corner.

With a heavy sigh, I turn and walk into the café, and am immediately enveloped in the smell of coffee beans and fresh baked pastries. If my stomach wasn't coiled with anxiety, it would be downright heavenly.

I swallow hard and keep walking, finding Brighton sitting at a round, two-person table in the middle of the room. Her eyes light up when she sees me coming toward her, and I smile, lifting my hand in a wave. She gets up and throws her arms around me when I reach the table.

"Why do I feel like I haven't seen you in a fucking year?" she asks, finally letting me go and dropping back into her chair.

I set my bag next to hers under the table and sit across from her. "I know, right? Sorry, things kinda sucked for a while. It's good to see you, though."

Her hazel eyes flick across my face as her brows knit. "You're really better?" she asks. "I was so worried about you."

I nod, reaching for her hands and giving them a quick squeeze. "I'm totally fine. I'm sorry I scared you."

She blows out a dramatic sigh. "Okay. You're forgiven. Because I love you and I desperately need to vent."

I laugh, arching a brow at her. "Yeah? Please feel free to go off. I'm all ears, Bri."

She shakes her head. "Food first, then I'll rant."

We grab lattes and croissants before returning to our table. I steal a quick glance around the café, wondering which of the other patrons are really the security team that's here to look out for me. It could be anyone—everyone looks the same in terms of casual street clothes and business attire.

Turning my attention back to Brighton, I wrap my fingers around the mug in front of me, lifting it to my mouth to take a sip of my vanilla latte. It's a bit sweet for my taste, but that's really not my main concern at the moment.

"What's going on?" I prompt her.

She shoves a chunk of pastry in her mouth. "Ugh. My dad. He made me move back in, claiming it was useless to pay for my apartment when he and my mom live in the city. Apparently he wants to spend more time as a family, which is complete bullshit."

I frown. "Why do you say that?"

"I've been back for almost a week and have seen him once. In passing. He's having all these closed door meetings and missing dinner every night. I tried talking to my mom about it, but she just brushes it off."

"He's having meetings at your house?" I ask over the rim of my mug, and she nods, tearing another piece off her croissant. "Is that abnormal? I mean, do you know what they're about?"

She stops chewing and stares at me for a few seconds. Long enough to make my stomach drop. Shit. I probably said too much.

Brighton finally shakes her head. "I haven't heard anything. Nothing that made sense anyway. I just... I'm worried about him. What if he's involved in something dangerous?"

I want nothing more than to comfort my best friend. Especially considering what I know about the things Scott Ellis is involved in. But I need to be very careful what I say.

"Listen," I tell her, "the term is almost over. Why don't we go away for the summer?" I figure I'll need to move around with the guys anyway, so why not have Brighton tag along? If it gets her away from the hunters, I want to make it happen—whatever it takes.

Her eyes widen. "Are you serious? Because I am so fucking down for that."

I nod. "Definitely. We can figure out the details later, but let's do it."

"Holy shit, yes," she shouts, earning a few looks from the people around us that she doesn't even notice. "When are you coming back to school?"

I bite into my croissant, chewing and swallowing before I answer her. "I fell pretty behind when I was sick, so I'm going to finish the term online. My professors have been accommodating, which has been great, but I do miss going to class."

She snorts. "Of course you do."

"I might actually see about transferring to remote courses for the fall term," I say.

Brighton shakes her head. "No. Absolutely not. I need you here, Cal." She looks seconds away from pouting, and I regret saying anything.

"It's not a for sure thing, I've just been thinking about it. I'd like to travel and see more of the world," I explain. "You can't tell me you've never thought about it."

She narrows her eyes at me, but eventually sighs. "Yeah, fine." A smile curls her lips. "Getting away for a while will be so nice," she comments.

"Definitely." I reach across the table and squeeze her hand. "And I get it. Parents can be… tough to deal with. Why do you think I moved away from mine?" I lean back and tear off a piece from my croissant, popping it into my mouth.

"Yeah, I guess. At least your dad isn't some shady businessman."

"Neither is yours, Bri," I lie through my teeth, the buttery pastry suddenly feeling heavy in my stomach. "Just because he has private meetings doesn't mean…" My voice trails off when her gaze abruptly drops away from mine. "Brighton," I say with an edge to my voice, my pulse kicking up. "What haven't you told me?"

She presses her lips together, and when she tilts her head back up, her eyes are glassy with unshed tears. "I… I lied to you before. I did overhear some things." The color leeches from her face and her chin quivers. "It didn't make any sense, but I… um, hacked into his email and found conversations with people that—" Her voice cuts off, and she whips her head around as if she's worried she'll be overheard.

And she will. By the vampire security team the guys sent me here with.

*Fuck, fuck, fuck.*

They'll report back and tell them what Brighton's telling me.

I reach back across the table, nearly knocking over my mug, and grasp her wrists, squeezing until she looks at me.

Her hazel eyes widen, and a single tear leaks down her cheek. "Calla—"

I shake my head, hoping she gets the message not to say anything else. "It's okay. I know you're not feeling well. Finals are stressing me out too."

Brighton frowns, her brows knitting, but finally nods. "Yeah, sorry." She sniffles.

"Hey, no worries." I hold her gaze. "Everything's going to be fine."

Her expression shifts to one filled with confusion, and I want nothing more than to explain everything to her. She knows more than we can discuss freely here, but I'm sure she —much like I do—has far more questions than answers at this point.

I stand, pushing my chair back. "I'll be right back, just going to slip into the washroom."

She nods in response, and I walk quickly through the café, the sounds of conversation, soft music, and the hiss of a milk steamer filling the space until I close the washroom door behind me, muffling all of it.

Leaning against the door, I flip the lock over and pull out my phone. My finger hovers over Atlas's name, and I bite my lip. Instead of texting him, I open my conversation with Brighton and type a quick message.

*Keep your eyes on your phone. Do not look up. We can't talk out in the open here.*

Her response comes a few seconds later.

*What the fuck, Cal?!*

*I'm sorry, but I need to know what you heard during your dad's meeting.*

The little text bubble pops up, then disappears, then returns. I hold my breath until her message finally comes through, and then my entire body fills with dread.

*I know about the vampires.*

## 5

# KADE

Lex drags my ass out of bed sometime after noon. The bastard. I was quite content to spend the whole fucking day here. While it's not the most comfortable bed—certainly nowhere near the mattress I was forced to leave behind at our place—I'm more exhausted than I'd care to admit. Despite drinking from Calla and sleeping all night, my muscles ache with tension and the thought of working out makes me want to ignore Lex in the doorway, roll over, and go back to sleep.

Atlas slept on the couch last night because he and Calla were heading to Washington this morning, so I stole the other half of the bed Lex crashed in.

"We have company," he mutters, pushing away from the doorframe, and snags my T-shirt off the floor, tossing it at me.

I catch it out of the air and sit up, raking my fingers through my hair before tugging my shirt on over my head and getting up to follow him into the hallway. "What the fuck are you talking about? No one is supposed to know we're here." My tone is sharp and my pulse ticks faster.

Whoever is here isn't human, otherwise I'd be able to smell their blood. I *do* smell blood, but it isn't fresh and there are about six different sources. We must've gotten blood bags while I was passed out.

"Relax. Come see for yourself."

Stepping into the kitchen, my eyes immediately land on Fallon where she leans against the counter, nursing a cup of tea. She's wearing a skin-tight black leather bodysuit with high-waisted jean shorts and mesh leggings. She looks downright stunning with dark makeup and her bright red corkscrew curls.

Fucking hell. Talk about a blast from the past.

"Kade," she says in greeting, though it's clear by her tone and the smile missing from her crimson-colored lips just how thrilled she is to see me. Evidently, my memories from the night we spent together decades ago are more fond than hers. Perhaps it's the morning after she recalls, when I left her in that hotel room to get back to the guys.

"Fallon," I reply, grinning at her as I cross my arms over my chest. "Long time no see, gorgeous."

She rolls her eyes and takes a sip of her tea. "Charming as ever, I see."

I shrug. "What can I say? Some of us are just born that way." I flick a glance to Lex before looking back at her. "What are you doing here?"

"I've been in contact with Marcel. He told me where you lot were hiding out, so I offered to stop by with some blood and see if there's anything I can do to help."

My eyes narrow on her. "Why would you do that?"

"Because I'm not an asshole?" she offers dryly, then adds in a serious tone, "Because I care about Gabriel." She sets the empty mug in the sink. "I know he's still with that psycho sire of his, but—"

"Not for long," Lex cuts in. "Atlas went to get him."

My gaze swings toward him. "He what?" We didn't talk about that last night. Lex and I were supposed to go with him.

Lex turns to me. "He decided it was best he go alone. He didn't want to risk all of us returning to Washington now that we have targets on our backs."

"And you just let him go?" I snap, my chest tightening. I want Gabriel back as much as he and Atlas do, but the thought of them both being in danger and us being stuck here makes me want to put my fist through a wall.

He blinks at me. "You expected me to stop him? To go against him?"

I growl in response, shaking my head at the ridiculousness of the whole fucking situation. "Fine. So what? We're just supposed to wait here until they come back? What about Calla?"

Lex shrugs. "She's meeting with Brighton, so I guess we'll have to face the outcome of that when she returns, presumably with Atlas and Gabriel."

"You are infuriatingly calm about this," I grumble.

"I recognize there's nothing I can do right now. I'm pissed, but getting all tense like you are now isn't going to change anything or help the situation."

I stare at him, then mutter under my breath, "Whatever."

Sliding around Fallon, I open the fridge and find it stocked with blood bags. I pull out a B-positive and pour it into a glass before popping it into the microwave to heat it up. Once the timer beeps, I take my breakfast and walk into the living room, dropping onto the couch and kicking my bare feet up on the coffee table.

Lex and Fallon join me a couple minutes later, chatting about some broadway show Lex saw the last time he was in New York, while I down the blood in my glass. I feel a bit stronger once I've finished it, but a blanket of lethargy still seems to cling to me.

My thoughts shift to my sister as I tune out of Lex and Fallon's conversation. As hard as I try to recall the last time I saw her before she disappeared—or we *thought* she disappeared—it's blurry. It was before I turned and it fucked me up so badly that thinking about it sends me to a dark place I really don't want to visit. Despite that, I need to know what happened to her and why the hell she's aligned herself with the very people who threaten her existence.

I shake my head, forcing myself to tune back into the conversation happening next to me.

"Have you heard anything from Jase?" Lex asks Fallon.

I arch a brow at her. "Who the hell is Jase?"

She flicks an annoyed glance my way and says, "He's my partner."

I can't help the smirk that forms on my lips. "Oh, really? And how did you two lovebirds meet?" She's so easy to get a rise out of, I can't help myself. Especially if it distracts me from thinking about... other things.

Fallon scowls, shaking her head. "For a century-old vampire, you're a fucking child, Kade." She turns her attention back to Lex, and I don't bother adding that I'm older than a century, because she's clearly done talking to me. "I spoke to him on my way here," she says. "He was heading to Washington to back Atlas up if needed." Her jaw sharpens when she clenches it, gripping the arms of the antique chair she's sitting in. "I wanted to go, to rip that blond bitch limb from limb, but Jase thought it was best he go instead." She rolls her eyes. "Something about keeping a level head or whatever."

Knowing there's another vampire going after Gabriel with Atlas makes me feel a bit better even though I've never met the guy. He's friends with Gabriel, which means he's one of the good ones—someone we can trust.

Fallon pulls her phone out, reading the screen, and her lips curl into a smile. "They've got him."

My stomach clenches, and I sit forward, staring at her. "What else did he say? What happened? Did they slaughter Selene?"

She shakes her head without looking up from her phone. "All he said is that they have Gabriel."

My eyes shift to Lex, who is reaching for his phone. "Atlas says they're on their way to pick up Calla and head back, but nothing about Selene."

Fuck. That means she's still alive.

"So now we have to sit around for at least three hours waiting for them. Great."

"You need a hobby," Fallon mutters, typing something on her phone.

I shoot her a dark glance even though she's not looking at me. "Oh, I have hobbies. I'm surprised you don't remember. Or maybe you do."

Her fingers freeze and she lifts her gaze to meet mine. "If I recall, you weren't much to remember."

Lex snorts.

I narrow my eyes at her, but before I can come up with a sharp retort, Lex curses, gripping his phone tight enough he's going to shatter the glass screen if he doesn't ease up.

I move over to him in a blur and pry it from his hands. My jaw clenches as I take in the alert from our security team, then I lift my gaze, shifting it from Lex to Fallon. "We have a problem."

## 6

## CALLA

The ugly beige bathroom walls close in on me. Black spots dance across my vision and there's a dim ringing in my ears.

I'm having a panic attack. Right now. Awesome.

Sweat dots my brow and my fingers shake as I struggle to type a response.

*When did you find out?*

I have no idea what else to say. This whole situation just got a million times more complicated.

*A week ago. How do YOU know about them?!*

*It's a long story.*

*One that has to do with Gabriel? I know he's a vampire. His name came up in the meeting my father was having. The vampire hunter meeting. Because apparently that's the family business my mom was so adamant I stay out of.*

I blink back tears as fear digs its claws deeper into my chest. I want to take Brighton away from all of this. She deserves this life about as much as I do. It isn't fair for either of us.

*Yes. There's a lot we need to talk about, but I can't stay in here and text you for the next half hour or my fanged babysitters are going to know something's up.*

*Calla, are you in trouble?*

I almost laugh at her message, because yeah. I'm in so much fucking trouble. And I'm about to make it a hell of a lot worse.

*I'm coming out,* I type back. *We need to get out of here and somewhere we can talk without being overheard.*

*My car is parked out front. When you come out, I'll get up, and we'll leave.*

There's a chance one of the vampires watching us will step in and try to stop me from leaving with Brighton, but I'm going to have to take that chance.

With a deep breath, I slide my phone into my back pocket and leave the bathroom. My pulse ticks faster the closer I get to the table, but I force myself to reach for my bag and smile at Brighton.

"Sorry to do this," I tell her, "but I have to get going. It was really great to see you, though. We have to get together again soon. Maybe after finals?"

She stands, shouldering her bag. "Definitely. I think I'm going to stick around and study for a bit, but I'll walk you out."

We walk out the front door, and Brighton pulls her keys out unlocking the car. She meets my gaze, and I nod at her. Without a word, we get into the car and she starts the engine, pulling away from the curb a moment later.

"Where am I supposed to go?" she asks, her voice shaking. She was able to keep it together in the café, but her hands are gripping the steering wheel so tight her knuckles are white. She's freaking out—rightfully so.

"Take a breath," I tell her in what I hope is a calming

voice, because I'm sort of freaking out too, but one of us needs to keep a level head. The last thing I need is for Brighton to lose her shit and crash the car. "Head toward the interstate."

She offers a tense nod. "Are you going to tell me what the hell is going on?"

"I told you about the vampires once," I say, watching the confusion pass over her face. "You don't remember because Kade glamoured you to forget."

Her gaze whips toward me and her voice cracks when she says, "What? What does that mean?"

I cringe inwardly as she turns her eyes back to the road. "Do you maybe want me to drive? What I'm about to tell you is pretty overwhelming."

"No," she says quickly, "just keep talking. I want to know everything."

I pull in a slow breath, inhaling through my nose, then exhaling through my mouth. And then I tell Brighton about the blood oath, the night the guys came for me, getting kidnapped by Selene, and everything in between.

Her eyes are filled with tears, and she blinks hard to clear her vision, making the tears roll down her cheeks. "Holy shit, Cal. I... I don't even know what to say. I'm so fucking sorry."

I blink at her. "*You're* sorry? What could you possibly have to apologize for? I'm the one who kept all of this from you."

Brighton sniffles. "Not by choice. I'm sorry I couldn't be there for you through all of that." She pulls one of her hands off the wheel and reaches for me, grabbing my hand and squeezing it. "But I'm here now." Taking her hand back, she wipes the wetness from her cheeks.

"I know, but you probably shouldn't be."

She nods. "Because my family are vampire hunters." Shooting me a wide-eyed look, she adds, "which is not as cool as one would think."

"Right," I say, jumping when my phone starts vibrating from where I dropped it in the cup holder. My heart leaps into my throat when I see Atlas's name on the screen.

"Do you need to get that?" Brighton asks warily.

I bite my lip. Atlas could be calling about Gabriel. Or, the more likely situation, he's calling to reprimand me for leaving the café with Brighton. I'm sure someone from the security team has alerted the guys to my departure by now.

In a split-second decision I'll probably regret later, I shut my phone off and offer her a tense smile. "There is nothing I would rather do less right now."

"Got it. So don't. But you need to tell me where I'm driving."

Before I can overthink it, I type the safe house location into the GPS attached to the dash. "Where's your phone?" I ask her, and she hands it to me. I promptly turn it off and put it next to mine in the cup holder. I can't take any chances that Brighton's dad could be tracking her phone.

My best bet now is to get back to the safe house with Brighton and convince Kade and Lex to take my side to help protect Bri from her family. It's a long shot, but I'm too anxious to think of something better at the moment. One thing at a time.

"Where exactly are we going?" she asks, glancing between the GPS and the road.

"Somewhere safe." I drum my fingers on my thighs in an attempt to distract myself and calm my nerves.

"Will there be vampires there?"

My fingers still against my leggings. "Kade and Lex. Atlas drove me to Washington and he's getting Gabriel back from his sire, though if I had to bet, he's managed that and knows I gave our security team the slip, which likely means he and Gabriel are headed this way as well." They may not be able to track my phone now, but I can't exactly turn off their connection to my blood.

"Right. So your plan is to take me—the daughter of a vampire hunter—to a house full of vampires?"

I look in her direction, pursing my lips. "They aren't going to hurt you. You are one of the most important people in my life. If anything, they'll help keep you safe."

"Safe," she says in a small voice, "from what?"

I frown. "Do your parents know that you know about the vampires and the hunters?"

She shakes her head, keeping her eyes on the road, and a fraction of the tension in my chest eases.

"What do you think would happen if they did?"

"Honestly, I have no idea. When mom was so adamant about me finding my own path or whatever to keep me out of the family business, I just thought she wanted me to follow my dreams. To give me a choice of what *I* wanted." She adjusts her grip on the wheel. "I keep thinking about what would've happened if I'd grown up knowing about vampires. If my mom hadn't kept me away from the hunters."

Nausea ripples through me. "You'd probably *be* a vampire hunter," I say in a gentle tone.

"Yeah. Instead, we're here." She laughs, but it doesn't hold any humor.

"I know you're probably scared and confused as hell right now, but for what it's worth, I'm glad your mom kept you out of it. Otherwise, we would've never met."

She smiles. "Considering the company you're keeping these days, that might not be true."

My eyes widen, but when she bursts into laughter —*genuine* laughter—I join in. "Very funny," I mutter.

Brighton sighs heavily, tipping her head back against the headrest. "This is so messed up, Cal."

"I know, but we're going to figure it out," I tell her, determination clear in my tone.

"Are you trying to convince me or yourself of that?"

My stomach sinks, and I offer a dry laugh. "Both I guess."

My nerves are at an all-time high when we pull into the driveway of the safe house.

"You're sure about this?" Brighton asks, her voice pitchy.

The front door opens and Kade marches outside, his expression grim. Well, shit.

"Too late now," I mutter, unbuckling my seat belt and reaching for the door. "Give me a sec."

Kade rips the door open from the outside before I can and hauls me out of the car. "Are you insane?" he growls in my face.

"Not the welcome I was hoping for."

He pulls me away from the car and toward the house. "What exactly were you hoping for by bringing her here and compromising our location?" His eyes flick to the car before returning to me.

I open my mouth, but whatever response I was going to use dies on my lips. "She needs our help, Kade. Besides, this place was supposed to be temporary, right?"

His eyes narrow sharply. "Not the point. Bringing her here was stupid."

"She's not a hunter."

"Not yet," he snaps. "She lives with them, though. And once her father finds out where she is—"

"She's not going to tell him," I shoot back.

"You think she'll have to? You think he doesn't have her phone tracked?"

I cross my arms over my chest. "Actually, no. I don't think

he has her phone tracked. As far as he knows, Brighton knows nothing about the vampires, which was true until she overheard him in a meeting. He doesn't know she knows," I say in a tense voice. "Plus, I turned our phones off."

He exhales slowly, looking past me to the car again. "Get inside. Now."

"Fine," I snap back. "Have you talked to Atlas? Did he get Gabriel?"

"You'd know he did if you answered your fucking phone."

"Are you done yelling at me?" I ask in a level voice.

"Oh, *I* am. Just wait until Atlas gets here."

I roll my eyes, but my pulse jumps at his words. Dealing with Atlas's wrath is going to be a special kind of hell. "What's his ETA?"

Kade purses his lips. "You've got forty-five minutes tops."

"Great," I mutter dryly, glancing toward the house. "Where's Lex?"

"He's inside with Fallon debating the most painful place to get tattooed."

I frown at the unfamiliar name. "Fallon?"

"Friend of Gabe's," he explains, walking backward toward the house. "You better not try to take off."

"Relax, Kade. We drove here, remember? I'm not going anywhere."

He stares at me a moment longer before turning and walking up the porch steps.

I flip him off before returning to the car to grab my bag. "Ready?" I ask Brighton.

She unbuckles her seat belt slowly. "That was intense."

I shrug. "It's all good. Come on."

We walk toward the house, and I can see the fear on Brighton's face. I wrap my arm around her shoulders as we climb the stairs onto the porch. "You're safe here. I promise."

She nods, and we step inside. I close the door behind us

and I drop my bag onto the bench against the wall of the foyer. I head down the hall toward the living room, Brighton following me hesitantly.

Lex gets up from the couch the second we step into the room. "You're in big trouble," he mutters, but instead of yelling at me as Kade did, he pulls me into his arms and kisses the top of my head.

I step back in surprise and nod at him. "So I've been told. Lex, this is—"

"Brighton Ellis," he answers for me. "We met at that house party last month."

Oh, yeah. I completely forgot about that.

"Hi again," she says in a nervous tone.

He grins at her, flashing his fangs, and Brighton gasps and steps back.

I elbow him in the ribs. "Don't start."

His fangs retract, and he shoots me a wink before returning to his place on the couch.

We walk into the living room, and my eyes land on a gorgeous redhead sitting with one black mesh stocking-clad leg over the other. Her silver eyes meet mine and her red lips curve into a small smile.

"Hey," I say, "it's Fallon, right?"

She nods. "It's nice to finally meet you, Calla. Gabriel speaks very highly of you."

Heat rushes to my cheeks, and I smile. "Thanks. It's nice to meet you too."

"I bet you'll be glad to have Gabe home. I was just texting my partner, Jase, who was with Atlas when they, uh, picked him up." Her eyes flit between Brighton and me. "Anyway, they should be here any minute."

My heart lurches. *Any minute?* I turn my gaze to Kade. *Forty-five minutes, my ass,* my glare in his direction says.

He smirks, offering a shrug in response.

As much as I'm looking forward to seeing Gabriel, I would quite literally rather do anything else instead of dealing with Atlas.

"Marcel just sent through the details for our new place," Lex says to Kade, showing him his phone.

Kade shrugs. "Not the same, but I guess it'll do for now."

Lex nods in agreement. "It's not forever."

"Do I get to see?"

"Nope," Lex says, popping the 'p'.

I scowl, shaking my head.

"Childish, aren't they?" Fallon offers with a faint grin.

"It's unbelievable," I agree.

Her eyes flash with excitement. "They're here."

My stomach drops, and I shift closer to Brighton as she tenses.

"Calla—"

"It's fine," I assure her, though I really don't know what's about to go down.

As expected, Atlas is the first one through the doorway into the living room. Completely unexpected, though, is Brighton pulling me away from him when he storms into the room.

"Leave her alone," she says to him, her voice cracking but her grip on my arm strong.

He easily pries her fingers off me in a second. "Sit down and shut the fuck up." His voice is smooth, scarily calm.

She does as she's told, her expression passive and her eyes glazed over.

My jaw clenches, but before I can yell at him for glamouring Brighton, he grabs my wrist and drags me down the hall, shoving me into the bedroom and slamming the door shut behind us.

"You ever do something that blatantly idiotic again, and I'll make sure you can't sit for a fucking week."

Is… is he threatening to spank me? I press my lips together, trying to stifle the burst of laughter trying to escape. Because that is the last thing this conversation needs. Atlas is pissed enough as it is. I'm well aware, but I don't know how else to respond to the thought of his palm cracking against my ass cheek.

He growls low in his throat, his eyes filled with the same fire expanding in my belly. "I can smell exactly how you feel about that." His voice is thick with arousal, which only makes my body heat more, a flush creeping across my chest.

"Go ahead," he taunts. "Test me. See where that will get you."

I narrow my eyes despite the pounding in my chest and swallow past the dryness in my throat. "Bent over your knee?"

My quip is rewarded with a dazzling smile, one that steals the breath from my lungs in a vicious *whoosh* and fills me with a swirling mix of fear and excitement.

He stalks forward, a predator hunting his prey, and I instinctively reach for the door handle. He steals my wrist before I can grasp it and lifts both wrists over my head, pinning them to the back of the door with one hand. His other hand grips my hip, holding me against the door.

"I thought about exactly what I was going to do to you the entire drive here," he says, his lips next to my ear.

My mouth goes dry. "Oh?" I force out. "And what did you decide?"

His responding chuckle stirs the hair at my temple, and I gasp when his hand moves from my hip, sliding under the waistband of my leggings, brushing my folds, and dips two fingers into me without warning.

"Interesting form of punishment," I say in a breathy voice, tipping my head back against the door as he pumps his fingers in and out at a languid pace, teasing my clit with this thumb.

His lips find my neck, and I turn my face to the side, baring it to him completely. An invitation in more ways than one. His fangs scrape along my skin, sending a shiver down my spine, and his swift bite steals my breath. He drinks deeply, his fingers curling inside me, driving me wild with a pleasurable mix of sensations.

I press my lips together in an attempt to muffle my moan, but it's still audible enough I blush, knowing everyone but Brighton will hear exactly what's happening in here. But right now, I can't find the will to care.

Once Atlas retracts his fangs and drags his tongue along the puncture marks to heal them, I turn my face toward his, capturing his lips with mine in a sensual kiss that I feel all the way to my toes.

He kisses me back hard, picking up the pace of his fingers in my pussy until I'm moaning without inhibition against his lips.

I'm racing toward climax, my head back against the door and my hips grinding against him.

And then he breaks the fiery kiss and pulls his fingers out of my heat mid-thrust.

"What the fuck?" I growl breathlessly, my chest heaving as I tug on my wrists, wanting to reach for him. "Keep going."

"No," he says simply.

"No?" I echo incredulously, shaking my head. "What, you want to watch me finish myself?" I tug on my wrists again. "Fine. Let go of me, and I will."

He grips my chin, holding me in place as I struggle against him. "You will not touch yourself until I allow it." The power of his glamour pours through me like ice in my veins, but it does nothing to ease the throbbing heat between my thighs.

He lets me go, stepping back and watching me with dark eyes.

I glare at him. "You're an asshole." Ripping the door open, I storm out of the bedroom, blinking past the burn of tears, willing them to recede as I walk back to the living room to see Gabriel.

Calla launches herself at Gabriel the minute she walks back into the living room. He catches her as though he was expecting it and wraps his arms around her waist, holding her to him as if his immortal life depends on it.

Lex watches them for a brief moment, a soft smile on his lips, then turns his attention to his phone. I'm hoping he's communicating with Marcel to confirm when we can move to our next residence, because I'd like nothing more than to get the hell out of this shack. I understand we won't be able to return to the home we built for some time—if ever—but there has to be something nicer than this place where we can stay while we figure this shit out.

I turn my gaze back to Calla and Gabriel and scratch the back of my neck. I guess we're going to ignore what just went down between Calla and Atlas in the other room. Cool.

When she pulls back, her hands clasp his face and they share a moment of just staring at each other before Lex clears his throat.

"Not to ruin what is a very touching reunion, but we've

got about a million and one problems to deal with right now."

Calla shoots him a dirty look before focusing on Gabriel again as if Lex didn't say anything. "Are you okay?" she asks him, her gaze roaming over him to check for herself.

His hands drop to her waist, and he nods, pressing a kiss to her forehead. "I'm okay, angel."

After another moment of her staring at him without a word, she finally nods, accepting his answer. "What happened to Selene?" The bitterness in her voice when she says the woman's name is something we all share. Same with the urge to rip the vampire apart and burn her to ash for how she tormented Calla and for everything she's done to Gabriel since turning him.

"Jase and I forced our way past her pathetic security team at the building, broke into her penthouse, where Gabriel was..." Atlas frowns, glancing toward him, and he nods, his expression grim. Atlas clears his throat. "Where Gabriel was being fed on by Selene. They were both so caught up in it, they didn't hear us coming until we were already inside. She shoved Gabriel aside and took off. Jase tried to stop her, while I tended to Gabe, but she got away." Atlas's voice is rough. "No matter, it'll make her death that much more enjoyable when we catch up to her."

My stomach is knotted, my chest filled with a sharp pressure I can only identify as rage. I want that psycho vampire dead as much as the others.

"We're all together again. That's the important thing for now," Gabriel says in a calm tone. "Selene will meet her end, I have no doubt about that."

I don't understand how he's being so chill about this, though he's always been the most level-headed of our group. He's probably just relieved to be back with us.

Atlas is silent and his jaw is locked tight.

"What now?" Lex chimes in. "Are we going searching for the bitch?"

I lean forward, resting my elbows on my knees. "Fallon was in contact with another vampire Selene sired and believes she fled Washington for Chicago, so her and Jase are headed that way to see if there's any merit to that intel before we make any further moves against her. There's no point in doing anything until we know for sure."

Calla glances around the room in surprise, clearly not having realized that Fallon was gone.

"She said to tell you goodbye," Brighton mentions from her spot on the couch.

Calla turns to her friend and nods. "Sorry, uh… about before."

"Everything okay?" she asks quietly, as if she thinks speaking softly will ensure that we—the room full of vampires—won't overhear.

Atlas snickers, and her eyes shift between Brighton and him before she nods again. "Fine." There's an edge to her voice that Brighton frowns at, but she doesn't push the subject.

The human might be smarter than I initially gave her credit for.

I slip out of the room as Calla walks to sit next to Brighton on the couch. Might as well give everyone a few minutes to get reacquainted before we dive into all the doomsday planning. I retreat to the bedroom I slept in last night to steal a moment of quiet, but before I can close the door, Gabriel appears in the doorway.

"Can I come in for a minute?" he asks.

I walk away from the door, leaving it open, and drop onto the end of the bed. I rake my fingers through my hair, then scrub them down my face as Gabriel closes the door and walks closer.

"How are you doing?" he asks. "I've been worried about you since I heard about Meredith's unexpected return."

"Ah, that's right. Gabriel Simmons, dreamwalker extraordinaire." I exhale on a laugh. "We should probably figure that out, huh?"

He offers me a wry smile. "I'll add it to the list." His expression turns serious. "Now answer my question."

With a sigh, I tell him, "I'm probably doing about as well as you are, Gabe. You were locked up with your psycho sire for days. I have a feeling I don't want to know the shit she put you through."

He waves me off and sits next to me. "Nothing I wasn't expecting and haven't been through before."

My jaw clenches. "Whatever it was, that was the last time it'll happen," I vow.

Gabriel nods. "Atlas is pretty upset that she got away. Between that and the stunt Calla pulled…" His voice trails off, and he shakes his head.

"Never a dull moment around here," I offer with a faint grin.

He chuckles. "That is most definitely true." Angling himself toward me, he meets my gaze and asks, "Have you found out anything else about your sister?"

The grin dies on my lips. "Nothing. I don't know how to go about getting in touch with her. Maybe if I knew who her sire is I could, but I didn't even know she turned."

"Right, of course."

"Did Selene mention anything about her?" I ask.

He shakes his head. "I only found out about the hunter attack on the house when I reached Calla in her dream."

"Right. Do you have any idea how you made that happen?"

He offers a light shrug. "All I did was focus on her, on the pull of our bond. It took a while because of how close I was to Selene. Our sire connection was overpowering. But there was a brief moment where I could feel Calla strongly, so I latched onto that, closed my eyes, and willed her to appear before me. I'm not going to sit here and pretend to know how it worked, but it did." He reaches over and rests his hand on my thigh in a comforting manner. "We can explore that later. I know the situation with Meredith is concerning. I can't imagine how you're feeling."

I glance down at his hand on my thigh and exhale a heavy breath, shocked at how much tension eases out of my shoulders at his touch. "I'm at a loss, Gabe," I admit, and I despise how weak my voice sounds. "She clearly hates me, considering she stabbed me in the chest with a white ash dagger, nearly hitting my heart." I swallow the lump in my throat, willing myself to get a fucking grip on my emotions. "All those years ago when she disappeared, I let our parents give up and bury an empty casket."

His fingers wrap around my knee and he squeezes until I lift my gaze to his. "None of that was your fault," he says in a firm voice. "None of it. You were a kid. She was gone for so long, there was no other viable option or anything else you or anyone else could have done at that point. Your family deserved closure."

My jaw clenches when my eyes start to burn. "Closure…" I echo the word, and it tastes like poison on my tongue. "She wasn't dead," I say through my teeth, sniffing sharply as my nose starts to run.

"But she did die," he says in a gentle tone, and he's right.

I nod, dread coiling around my chest like a snake, putting pressure on my lungs and making it hard to breathe. "And now she wants to kill me."

"You don't know that for sure," he points out. "She had a chance to but she didn't. That could mean something."

"Yeah, that she wants me to suffer before the hunters—or

*her*—next attack." Even as I say the words, I don't exactly believe them. Despite her attack a few days ago, I can't see Meredith that way. She was never cruel or vicious. She was warm and kind. The type of person that would do anything for the people she cared about. Becoming a vampire, it wouldn't have destroyed that part of her. Even as I sit here with my head spinning, I cling to that. I have to believe it, because the alternative is too fucking devastating to consider. Because if my sister truly hates me... I don't know how I'll live with that.

Gabriel frowns. "Or," he says pointedly, "she's angry but still wants an opportunity to know her brother. Don't you think it's worth finding out?"

I sigh and mutter, "Your optimism can be so fucking annoying sometimes."

He smiles, bumping my shoulder with his. "I missed you too, Kade."

❦ 8 ❦

## CALLA

I'm not a vampire, but even I can sense the anxiety rolling off Brighton in waves. Her knee bounces erratically as she chews her bottom lip, staring at the unlit fireplace.

I want to comfort her, to reassure her that everything is going to be fine. She's an adult; she doesn't have to return to Washington—or her family of vampire hunters—if she doesn't want to. As much as I want to keep her with us, that likely won't fly. Brighton trusts the guys as much as they trust her, and keeping her with us would be a hell of a liability, especially if Scott decides to track her down.

With a sigh, I reach over and wrap my hand around her knee, stilling it. "Are you hungry?" I ask softly.

It takes her a second to pull her gaze away from the fireplace and look at me. Her eyes are glassy with unshed tears, and she shakes her head.

"I sure am," Lex chimes in from where he's sitting across from us.

"You know where the fridge is," I tell him without turning my attention away from Brighton.

"Yeah, but I prefer the fresh stuff," he says, and I catch him rising from his seat out of my peripheral.

Brighton stiffens next to me, and I squeeze her knee reassuringly before shooting Lex a glare. "Don't even think about it."

He pouts. "You're no fun." He saunters out of the room, and Brighton finally relaxes a little once he's gone. Fair enough. I understand her unease. Lex is… rather intimidating if you don't know him. Hell, even if you do. His wild eyes and chaotic demeanor still make me nervous a lot of the time. He won't hurt me, that I'm sure of, but besides that, I have no idea what he'll do sometimes.

My eyes flick to Atlas, who has been sitting silently since Kade and Gabriel left the room. His eyes are closed as if he's sleeping, but I have no doubt that he's awake and listening to everything happening around him.

"When are we leaving here?" I ask.

His chest rises and falls with a deep breath, but he doesn't open his eyes. "Once I've decided what to do with your friend."

Brighton sucks in a short breath but doesn't dare say anything.

I offer her a look that I hope says *it's okay*. "I think she should come with us."

His lips twitch, and he opens his eyes, his gaze slicing through me, heating my body with thoughts of what happened between us less than an hour ago. "Is that right?" He rubs his jaw, scratching the stubble there. "Because what could possibly go wrong if we take the daughter of one of the top vampire hunters in the country? Let me think about that for a second." His gaze darkens. "She's not coming."

Lex returns to the living room with a blood bag in his hand. He pulls the plastic topper off and brings it to his lips, shooting a wink at Brighton. He's clearly trying to freak her out, and based on the color draining from her face and her hands shaking in her lap, it's working.

"Seriously?" I snap at him.

He shrugs and continues drinking.

"Ignore him," I tell Brighton.

"Mean," he grumbles, dropping into the chair on the other side of the fireplace and kicking his booted feet on the coffee table. "Can't we just glamour the squirmy one and get on with our lives?"

"No," I say in a harsh voice. "I'm not going to let you mess with her head again."

"I… I won't tell anyone anything," Brighton says in a small voice. "I don't want to be part of anything my family is involved in, I swear. I wish I hadn't found out about it to begin with."

"That would certainly make our lives easier," Kade says as he and Gabriel walk back into the living room. It's not a large room, so having four vampires and two humans really takes the claustrophobic feel to the next level.

I angle my body toward Brighton, while Gabriel grips the back of the couch behind me. As opposed to Lex, Gabriel's presence is calming, reassuring. "Do you want to forget?" I ask her in a soft voice, knowing the guys would be more than willing to oblige wiping her memories.

"Y-yes," she answers in a voice barely above a whisper without meeting my gaze. She lets out a heavy sigh before looking at me. "But I don't want you to go through this by yourself. So, I'm not going to forget. I'm going to be here for my best friend." She reaches for my hands, squeezing them in hers.

"That's touching and all," Lex says, his lips red with blood, "but not your choice. It would be stupid of us to let you go knowing what you do."

"Why?" I push. "The hunters already know you're vampires."

"They may know we're vampires but they don't know about you being with us," Atlas says, "and I'd like to keep it that way."

"We could always send her back to spy on her daddy for us," Kade offers with a bored expression.

I shoot him an incredulous look and shake my head for added measure. "No. Absolutely not."

"We're not going to do that," Gabriel says in a level voice, and a bit of the panic in my chest eases.

"Well, whatever," Kade grumbles. "I don't think we should let her leave without wiping her memories."

"Enough," Atlas calls out, snaring the attention of everyone in the room. "We are not discussing this anymore. Brighton will go back to Washington and live as she did before today's events." His gaze focuses on her, and I can tell by the swirling of his silver irises he's about to glamour her. "You will drive straight home and tell no one what happened today. You will not share this location. You and Calla never left Washington. You sat at the café and commiserated over the big, bad vampires, and then you went home. You will not, under any circumstances, say a word about what you know to anyone outside of this room. Do you understand?"

"I understand," she says automatically.

"Good." He turns his gaze on me, and I narrow my eyes at him. He better not fucking glamour me right now. "Say goodbye to your friend," he says, though his words aren't weighted in glamour.

Brighton and I get up from the couch, walking toward the front door. Once we're outside in the driveway, I wrap my arms around her. I'd like nothing more than to have her stay, to keep her away from the man she calls Dad. But I've lost this fight. It makes me want to scream or cry—or both, honestly. I wish I'd fought harder, but the worst part is, we would've ended up here regardless. The guys will never trust Brighton, same as she'll never trust them. I have nothing to do with it on either side.

"Let me know when you get home, okay?" I say, pulling back. "Oh, and don't turn your phone on until you're back in the city."

She offers me a watery smile and nods. "I'm scared to leave you here." Her eyes shift past me toward the house.

I sigh, understanding her concern. If the roles were reversed, I'd be going crazy with worry. "They won't hurt me," I promise her. "I know things are messed up right now, but they... they're not so bad." I laugh softly, almost to myself. It's wild that just over a month ago, I hated them—I genuinely wanted to *kill* them. And now... I don't know. Things have definitely changed. I'm not exactly sure how I feel about that, and now doesn't quite seem like the time to figure it out. Perhaps when we're not running from vampire hunters while simultaneously hunting a vampire ourselves.

Brighton gets behind the wheel and starts the car, rolling down her window.

"Be careful," I tell her, hugging my arms around myself.

She nods. "You too, babe. We'll talk soon." She slides her sunglasses on and rolls the window up before backing her car down the gravel drive.

I stand there long after her car has disappeared from view.

"You should come back inside."

Gabriel's gentle voice startles me, and I turn around to face him. "This is such a fucking mess, Gabriel." I clench my jaw against the tears burning my eyes.

He tilts his head, regarding me thoughtfully before closing the distance between us in a few smooth strides. "I know, angel." He reaches for me, running his hands up and down my arms, then tucks me against his side, guiding me back toward the house.

Back inside, I grab Gabriel's hand and pull him down the hallway into the bedroom I've been occupying before I can think too much about what I'm doing.

The corner of his mouth kicks up and his bright silver eyes glimmer with amusement. "What are you doing?"

"I'm going to show you how much I missed you, and you are going to distract me from the shit storm that has become our lives." Atlas glamoured me so I can't touch myself to get off. He said nothing, however, about one of the others making me come. I tug my shirt off, tossing it to the side and kicking off my shoes before adding, "Any objections?"

He steps closer, trailing his fingers up my arms and along my collarbones until his hands are cupping my neck, holding me in place. "Absolutely none." He captures my lips in a slow, sensual kiss that leaves me tingling everywhere, heat gathering low in my belly. Pulling me against him, he tips my head back, deepening the kiss as his tongue sweeps across my bottom lip, seeking entrance.

I open to him, grazing my tongue along his and gripping the front of his shirt in my fists. He drops his hands to my hips and lifts me off the floor without breaking the kiss. I wrap my legs around him, gasping into his mouth when I feel his hardness against me. His lips curve against mine as he carries me to the bed, laying me down and hovering over me. His lips part from mine, and he drags his mouth down my throat and chest, between my breasts, making my breath hitch as he quickly moves lower, flicking his tongue against the skin above my navel.

My body is still wound tightly from Atlas's attention and denial earlier, so it takes very little time for heat to gather between my thighs, especially with the way Gabriel is looking up at me through his lashes, as if I'm truly an angel like he calls me.

I press my lips together, watching him pull my leggings down all the way to my ankles, letting them drop onto the floor at the end of the bed before he drops his mouth to the inside of my thigh. I squirm as his lips get closer to my center, and he shoots me a faint grin that says *keep still*.

I nod, shifting up the bed a little so my head rests against the pillows.

The first pass of his tongue along my slit vaults my hips off the mattress as I suck in a sharp breath.

"Easy," he murmurs, gliding his hands up my thighs, spreading them open before trapping my hips so I can't move them again.

I catch my bottom lip between my teeth, keeping my eyes on him as he lowers his mouth back to my core, flicking his tongue against my clit once, twice, three times before he sucks the bundle of nerves into his mouth, swirling his tongue around. I moan deeply, my eyes fluttering shut as his hands slide up my stomach, cupping my breasts through my bra.

I unclasp it, letting my breasts spill out, and his fingers quickly find my nipples, teasing them into hard peaks. I reach down and run my fingers through his copper hair, holding him against my pussy as he devours me.

"Fuck," I moan, my head spinning with ecstasy.

Gabriel takes his time tasting me. Switching from circling my clit with his tongue to licking my folds, dipping inside my tight channel before returning his attention to the bud at my center.

My chest rises and falls quickly as he continues his ministrations, massaging my breasts as I grip the sheets with one hand and his hair with the other.

He groans against my sex, sending vibrations through me,

and my pussy walls clench around his tongue, stealing my breath as I come, moaning his name. Gabriel laps up my release, sucking my overly sensitive clit before crawling up my body and sealing his lips over mine.

I taste myself on his mouth, which makes my core tighten with arousal. That paired with the way he's pressing his erection between my legs has me reaching for his shirt, tugging it off and tossing it toward the end of the bed. I waste no time going for his pants, undoing the button and zipper.

"Slow down," he murmurs against my lips.

"I need you," I breathe, sliding my hand into his pants and wrapping my fingers around his thick length. "I think you need me too."

He groans into my mouth. "Always."

In the time it takes me to blink, Gabriel stands and removes his pants before bracing himself over me again.

Okay, so I don't hate vampire speed all the time.

"Hmm, this looks like fun."

I gasp in surprise, leaning up on my elbows to find Lex and Kade in the doorway. "Jesus," I mutter.

"Hardly," Kade remarks dryly.

"Need a hand, brother?" Lex asks, looking at Gabriel and flicking his tongue over his bottom lip.

Gabriel looks down at me, his expression soft. "What do *you* want, angel?"

My eyes widen slightly, and I bite my lip, considering all the things these three could do to bring me pleasure. "I… I'd like them to join us," I say in a quiet voice, my cheeks flushing hotly.

His lips curl into a smile, and he leans down to press a gentle kiss to my lips. "You don't need to be embarrassed."

"Don't worry," Kade says, approaching on my right while Lex comes around to the other side. "Soon the only thing you'll feel is pleasure."

Lex and Kade slide into the bed on either side of me. Kade curls his finger around my chin, turning my face to him and claiming my mouth. My eyes flutter closed as Lex lowers his mouth to my breast, licking and sucking gently while massaging the other with his hand, rolling the nipple between his fingers and making me moan against Kade's lips.

"Her pussy is all yours, Gabe," Lex says with a smirk against my skin that fills me with heat.

Kade reaches between my legs, strumming my clit as Gabriel positions the head of his cock at my entrance. He pushes in slowly, stretching me around his thick length, and my thighs clench around him.

"Relax, angel," he says in a lust-filled voice.

Kade works my clit, pushing his tongue into my mouth as Gabriel's cock slides in further. My pussy grips him tightly, and Kade moves his mouth to my neck, kissing and sucking the sensitive skin below my ear, distracting me from the pressure between my legs as Gabriel pushes the rest of the way into me.

I take a minute to catch my breath, overwhelmed by the combination of sensations happening all over my body.

"Feeling left out?" Lex asks after pulling his lips off my breast.

I blink my eyes open and frown in confusion before I look to the doorway where Atlas is leaning, his arms crossed over his chest and his eyes lit with arousal. I drop my gaze and suck in a breath at the obvious bulge in his pants.

"It's a bit crowded in this tiny ass bed, but I'm sure we can make it work," Kade says.

Atlas walks into the room, but instead of coming toward the bed, he lowers himself into the chair by the window.

Lex chuckles. "Problem solved. Enjoy the show."

Atlas keeps his eyes on me as he reaches for the button on

his pants. Slowly, he unbuttons them, dragging the zipper down and pulling his cock free.

*Holy shit.*

Gabriel moves inside me, stealing my attention, and I press my lips together, moaning softly. He pulls halfway out before pushing back in slowly, steadily. He does it a few more times as my eyes drift back to Atlas, to where he's pumping his hand up and down his erection. Gabriel's pace is driving me mad, but I'm so caught up in watching Atlas, I can't make my lips move to tell him to go faster.

"Calla," Kade murmurs, nipping my earlobe.

Cue the full body shiver. "Mmm."

He drags his tongue along my neck. "I'm going to bite you."

My pussy clenches around Gabriel's cock, my heart racing with anticipation.

His chuckle stirs the hair at my temple. It's the only warning I get before his fangs sink into my skin, and I cry out in a mix of pleasure and pain.

Gabriel increases the speed of his thrusts, while Kade drinks deeply and continues circling my clit with his fingers. I reach for Lex, finding the front of his pants while keeping my gaze locked on Atlas. My fingers slide past the waistband and wrap around his hot, throbbing erection.

He hisses through his teeth, guiding my hand up and down his shaft at the pace and pressure he wants. "Fuck, that feels so good."

My muscles clench and heat floods through me, drowning my body in pure pleasure. I succumb to the building pressure between my thighs, my pussy clenching around Gabriel's cock as I come hard, crying out, my heart pounding against my chest so fast I'm almost concerned I'll pass out from too much stimulation.

Kade licks my neck, sealing the puncture marks as Gabriel slows his pace.

"No," I breathe, "keep going. You need to come."

"Calla," he groans, his eyes closed and his face filled with pleasure as he drives into me over and over. His muscles tense a few thrusts later as an orgasm rips through him.

Kade kisses me again, blocking my view of Atlas, but his deep grunts fill the room, mixing with Lex's as my hand continues to pump his erection. He tenses, shooting his release onto my hand a moment later.

Gabriel pulls out of me and disappears for a few seconds, coming back with a warm washcloth and cleans between my legs, making me tingle and shiver, my skin still very much sensitive.

Kade kisses my shoulder while Lex cleans our hands and tucks himself back into his pants. I turn my gaze to find Atlas doing the same.

The room is filled with our combined breathing, the smell of sex heavy in the air.

I yawn, curling onto my side and facing Kade, ready for a week-long nap. Gabriel slides in behind him while Lex presses against my back, resting his hand on my hip and his chin on my shoulder.

The sound of Atlas's ringtone makes me lift my head to see him pulling his phone out of his back pocket.

He sighs as if whoever is calling is the last person he wants to talk to, then gets up without a word, giving me one last look filled with something I can't begin to decipher before he's gone.

# KADE

Calla and Gabriel get dressed before the four of us find Atlas in the living room, tossing his phone onto the coffee table none too gently. The air in the small room is thick with tension, and his expression is grim, making me wish I'd listened in on the conversation from the bedroom.

I drop onto the couch with Lex while Calla perches on the armrest of the chair Gabriel sits in. If I was him, I'd pull her onto my lap in a second. He has far more self-control than I do.

"What was that about?" Calla asks, watching Atlas with a concerned expression. Her cheeks are still flushed, and the sight sends blood straight to my cock. *Fuck*. I need to focus. I tear my gaze away from Calla, focusing on Atlas.

He thrusts his fingers through his dark hair, leaning back against the chair as he rests his ankle on the opposite knee. "I'm being summoned," he says, shaking his head with a single, humorless laugh.

My lips turn down into a frown. This isn't the first time

Atlas has been summoned in the time I've known him. And it's never for anything good.

Calla's brows lift; of course she has no idea what's going on.

"So I guess we *are* going to New York," Lex says, picking at a hangnail on his thumb and shifting where he sits. He's connected to Atlas on a more physical level, which means he's likely experiencing some of the discomfort rippling through Atlas right now. I feel for him.

"Wait, what?" Calla cuts in, her eyes wide as she looks from Lex back to Atlas.

He lets out a heavy sigh. "My parents have requested an audience."

She shakes her head, crossing her arms. "They can't call you? What century are they living in?"

Lex snorts, and I press my lips together against a smile. I can count the number of times I've been in the company of Atlas's parents in the last few decades. They are stiff, old-school vampires, but they are powerful and scary as hell. The last thing we need is to get on their bad side. When they call, Atlas goes.

He blinks at her, clearly unamused. "It doesn't work that way." He looks past her to Gabriel, then to me and Lex, and continues, "I'm not the only one being summoned. They've called a summit. All born vampires from the main bloodlines are required to attend, otherwise they must send a proxy."

"Why now?" I ask. "What's happening that they need to bring everyone together?"

"There have been a string of vampire deaths across North America. Far more than we normally see, even with the increased number of hunters. It's starting to garner atten-tion. Many of the older born vampires want to wipe out the hunters to protect their own. They don't care that some of those vampires they want to protect are the same ones who needlessly kill humans for food and for sport."

"I'm going with you," Lex says, his gaze locked on his sire. His pulse is uneven and sweat dots his brow. The poor bastard is nervous. I want to reach over and clap my hand on his shoulder, to offer him comfort, but it'll make him uncomfortable. Lex despises feeling weak just as much as I do.

"No," Atlas says, holding his gaze, "you're not. You need to stay with your brothers and Calla."

"Uh, here's an idea," Calla chimes in, "how about we all go? I don't exactly have a desire to visit my home city, but it seems like the best option. I think we should stay together." She swallows, glancing at her lap for a moment before lifting her gaze to look at Atlas. "You shouldn't have to go alone."

His eyes flick across her face for a moment, his lips set in a tight line. "This isn't up for debate or discussion, Calla. I am going to New York to attend the summit, and the rest of you will stay put and prepare to move to the next safe house."

"I agree with Calla," Lex says in a low voice, and the room falls silent.

Calla is wide-eyed, staring at Lex; she's surprised to have someone taking her side in the conversation. Hell, I'm as surprised as she is, mostly that Lex would say anything to go against Atlas. I don't think that's happened in, well, ever.

Atlas inhales slowly. "Lex, do not—"

"There's no reason we shouldn't go with you," Lex says, cutting him off, and I can see it in his face that he's worried about being away from his sire.

"I can think of several," Atlas barks back.

"You should have backup," Calla says. "You guys protect me with security teams and whatnot. While it's annoying, it's also comforting."

"He isn't in danger," Gabriel assures her. "While these

*events* aren't pleasant, they aren't dangerous for someone like Atlas to attend."

She mulls that over. "Then what's the big deal if we come along?" Calla chimes in, facing Atlas. "Haven't you ever heard of moral support? This is the perfect example of a time when it would be helpful."

"What would be helpful is if you'd—"

"Atlas," Gabriel cuts in gently.

His jaw works, and he shoves a hand through his hair, exhaling a harsh breath. "I'll be gone very briefly. There's no sense in dragging you lot there when all you'll be doing is sitting in a hotel room. There are hunters everywhere. New York is one of the highest populated, so it's not as if you three can galavant through Times Square."

"Well, damn. There goes my plan," Calla remarks dryly, rolling her eyes.

Atlas shoots her a dark look. "I'm going alone. End of discussion."

Lex drops his gaze, frowning, but doesn't argue further.

"When do you leave?" I finally ask, knowing there's no sense continuing to try and convince him to let us go with him. That door is shut and locked.

"First thing in the morning, so if you all don't mind, I'm going to pack a bag," he says, getting up and walking out of the room.

Calla frowns, looking at Gabriel, who offers her a reassuring smile.

"Come on," he says, standing and guiding her up as well. "Let's see what we can find to make for dinner."

The two of them head into the kitchen, leaving Lex and I alone.

"Well, fuck," he mutters.

"Agreed," I say and I can't help but fear this is the beginning of a lot worse to come.

❧ 10 ❧

# CALLA

**M**arcel must've had clothing delivered while I was in Washington, because when I stop in front of the room the guy's have been sleeping in, Atlas is standing at the end of the bed, folding a pair of black dress pants into a duffle bag. His back is to me, but even from across the room I can't help noticing the tension in his shoulders. I mean, Atlas is tense on a good day, but this is different.

"Are you going to continue staring at me from the hallway?" he asks without otherwise acknowledging my presence.

I purse my lips, considering it for a moment before I step into the room and close the door. Kicking off my shoes, I walk over and crawl onto the bed, sitting cross-legged in front of him, the duffel bag between us. I pull at a loose thread on the worn duvet as he shoves a small stack of T-shirts into the bag.

"Something you want to say to me?"

My fingers freeze. I lick the dryness from my lips. "Do

your parents know what happened in Washington? The hunter attack on the house, I mean."

"Of course."

"But they don't understand why you might want to stay close to your friends, whether it be here or us joining you in New York?"

"It doesn't matter." His voice is clipped but level.

"Doesn't it?" I'm not sure why I'm pushing it. Maybe part of me hates the power the born vampires seem to have even just over their own kind. That, or maybe I don't want Atlas to leave.

He grips the duffle bag in his fist and practically rips the zipper shut before meeting my gaze. "No, Calla, it doesn't. I have responsibilities. I don't get to choose not to attend because I'd rather stay with my brothers and my—"

"Your *what?*" I cut in, my voice sharper than I was expecting. "What am I to you, Atlas?" I clamp my mouth shut when his blazing silver gaze slams into me. I have no idea where that came from and I certainly don't think I'm prepared to hear the answer, whatever it may be. "Forget it," I rush to say and move to get off the bed, but before my feet can reach the ground, Atlas is there, pinning me flat on my back against the mattress with his fingers locked around my wrists. My heart lurches in my chest as I watch his jaw work, and he glares down at me, his dark hair falling into his face. I have the urge to reach up and brush it back, but he has effectively immobilized me.

"Let me go." My racing pulse and the heat gathering between my legs are really out here trying to make a liar out of me.

"No."

My eyes narrow, and I mutter, "Fine. Then kiss me, you asshole."

The corner of his mouth curls into a wicked smirk. "Earn it."

I blink at him. "What the hell?"

"You heard me." He cocks his head to the side. "Fight me off, and perhaps then I'll give you what you clearly desire." His gaze lowers to where my shirt has ridden up, exposing my stomach.

Warmth floods my chest and cheeks. "Fuck you."

"Precisely." Amusement shines in his eyes as his grip on my wrists tightens. "I'll admit, I've missed our training sessions. It's only been a few days, but I found myself looking forward to them."

I roll my eyes but don't say anything. Because I can't disagree with him. I looked forward to them as well—too damn much. "You're saying this is some impromptu training session?"

"Oh, no." He leans down, pressing his body to mine, his lips at my ear when he says, "This is very real." When he leans back, his eyes are darker and his fangs flash in the light overhead.

I resent the shiver that zips through me. I cover it up with a scowl, thrusting my hips as hard as I can manage in an effort to buck him off. Instead, he lifts my arms above my head, laying me across the mattress so we're parallel with the headboard. His knee presses dangerously close to the throbbing at my core. I inhale and exhale short breaths, glaring up at him where he hovers over me, his gaze trained on my mouth.

"You're making this too easy," he says with a tsk.

My eyes fall to the dagger strapped around my thigh before flicking back to his face. I tug on my wrists until my skin burns under his grip. "Care to provide any advice?" I say through my teeth, my tone laced with bitterness.

"No."

"Do you just like saying that?" I shoot back, stilling beneath him.

His lips twitch. "I told you this wasn't a training session. If I was any other vampire, you'd be drained by now."

"If you wanted my blood, Atlas, all you had to do was ask." The words are out of my mouth before I can stop them.

"Actually, *Calla*, I don't." His mouth is against my neck in the time it takes me to blink, and I suck in a breath as his fangs scrape my skin. "I could do anything to you." He lowers his voice. "And the best part?" His knee inches higher, making my pulse jackhammer as his breath tickles my skin. "You'll let me because you want it."

"No," I breathe. I *lie*. I won't say it—I refuse to give him the satisfaction despite the moisture soaking through my panties, which he can no doubt smell. Fucking vampire senses.

"No," he echoes with a soft chuckle, his lips tracing the shell of my ear. "So if I were to bury my fingers between your thighs right now, I wouldn't find you absolutely fucking soaked for me?"

Holy hell.

I close my eyes, turning my face away. I'm not sure how long I can keep this up, denying what my body craves, even if there's a part of me that hates it.

"Ah, ah, ah. None of that. Look at me." His voice settles over me like a weighted blanket, and I comply without hesitation, his glamour clinging to me and controlling me effortlessly.

When he pulls back, our eyes meet, and I say, "Is this what you want?" I lick my lips. "Me, powerless beneath you, succumbing to your will?"

Atlas's jaw clenches into something sharp enough to cut glass and his eyes search my face as if it holds the answers to his prayers. "You—" He clears his throat. "You have no fucking idea."

I nod, forcing myself to hold his gaze. "Show me."

His mouth is on mine before I can think about what I've asked for. He devours me, his lips moving against mine, coaxing them to part for him, his grip on my wrists loosening ever so slightly. But it's enough.

I bring my leg up, slamming my knee into his stomach as hard as I can as I rip my wrists from his grasp. I roll away, right off the damn bed, landing hard on my hip. I wince as I force myself to my feet, reaching for my dagger before I'm even fully upright.

My eyes snap to the bed where I expect Atlas to be, but it's empty. I whip around, holding the dagger in front of me, and find him standing what has to be less than an inch from the tip of my blade. I start to step back, but he grabs my arm, holding me there.

I open my mouth to ask him what the hell he's doing, but he shakes his head, making the words die on my lips.

"You had me. Don't back down now."

*You had me.*

His words fill my chest with a somewhat unfamiliar warmth—pride. I got the upper hand. I tricked him and got away. But he's right, whatever upper hand I gained, I just lost it. Great.

I blow out a heavy breath. There's no chance I'm going to pull anything over on him now. "I'm calling it."

Atlas tilts his head to the side slightly. "Why?"

"This would be the part where I'd stab you if—"

"If what?" he cuts in, a challenging glint in his eyes. "If you didn't secretly care about hurting me?"

My eyes narrow and my grip on the hilt of the dagger tightens. I could remind him of the time, mere weeks ago, when I *did* stab him. Instead, I say, "Hardly. You don't even like me. Why would I give a shit about you?"

He laughs, shaking his head again.

"What?" I snap, lowering my arm with the dagger, and secure it back in its holder. We both know I'm not going to use it.

His eyes dance across my face. "You really believe that, don't you?"

I arch a brow, thrown by the softness in his voice. "When people show me who they are, I tend to believe them." And he's shown me more than once.

Atlas nods, his expression turning into something I mistake as thoughtful. Because then he says, "Is that why you let me fuck you against that tree?"

My cheeks fill with heat and my chest tightens, anger flaring to life in me. "I let you *fuck* me because I knew I needed to get you out of my system."

He smirks faintly. "I see. And did you?"

"Completely," I lie through my teeth without missing a beat.

"Right," he murmurs, stealing the distance between us with a single stride. "That's not nearly as convincing when I can hear the blood rushing through your body and your heart beating like a hummingbird in your chest. Not to mention the smell of your arousal."

I shrug, feigning indifference as I work really freaking hard to ignore the pull of desire urging me to grab the front of his shirt and kiss him until I can't think straight.

"Go ahead," he says, "tell me I'm wrong, that you didn't enjoy what I did to you this morning, and I'll forget the whole thing."

I swallow hard, but it doesn't help. "I don't know," I say, apparently deciding to add fuel to this fire, "It wasn't all that memorable."

My stomach swirls with nerves and heat as his lips slowly curl into a smile.

"Shame," he says, reaching for me before I can even consider moving away. He cups the side of my neck to hold me in place, his fingers warm against my skin. "Perhaps you need a reminder." He leans in, dipping his face until our foreheads are touching, and closes his eyes. I hold my breath, preparing for him to kiss me or bite me. Truth be told, I'm not sure which I crave more at the moment.

"Atlas," I whisper, my stomach pooling with warmth. I can't deny how much my body craves him for much longer.

His thumb brushes the pulse at my neck, and his throat bobs when he swallows. "You have one chance to walk out of here, otherwise you're mine for the night. I will not let you go."

I drag in a shallow breath, dropping my facade of indifference. "I'm here," I say in a low voice, gripping the front of his shirt. "I'm not leaving."

His chest rumbles with a low growl, his grip on my neck tightening a moment before he slants his mouth over mine, claiming me completely with a single fucking kiss.

I return the kiss with a fierce intensity, as if I need to prove something to him. Easing my grip on his shirt, I slide my hands up his chest and drape my arms over his shoulders, pushing my fingers into his hair as he tips my head back, deepening the kiss.

My world narrows on the sensations he's wringing from me. I am utterly consumed by this wicked vampire, and there's not a thing I can do about it—nothing I *want* to do. Nothing but this.

Without warning, his hands drop to my hips, and he lifts me without breaking the kiss. My muscles tense at the sudden movement, and the next thing I feel is the mattress at my back. His lips leave mine, giving me a chance to catch my breath as my eyes fly open to find him leaning over me, his hands pressing into the mattress on either side of me. His legs cage mine in where they dangle off the end of the bed, and when he straightens, moving his hands to the waistband of my leggings and peeling them down to expose my center, my heart races. He steps back, pulling each of my legs out to remove my leggings before kneeling before me.

The sight of Atlas York kneeling between my legs is something that will remain branded in my memory. Because holy shit, it is *hot*.

His hands glide up my legs slowly, his lips trailing after them, peppering kisses and making my skin tingle. He spreads my thighs, holding them open, and the moment his lips brush my folds, I tremble with need.

My chest is splotchy and warm, rising and falling quickly as I keep my eyes on the top of his head.

Atlas drags his tongue along my slit, circling my clit before sucking it into his mouth. He moans, sending vibrations directly to the bundle of nerves in his mouth, and I suck in a sharp breath, gripping the sheets and biting my lip.

He pulls back, resting his chin on my mound. "You still want to pretend you don't remember what I feel like inside you?"

I shoot him a glare. "Shut the fuck up and put your mouth back on me."

He graces me with a faint grin. "You're in no position to make demands." In a second, he has my hips trapped against the mattress. "You'll take what I give you and say thank you."

I open my mouth to shoot a retort back, but before the words have a chance to leave my mouth, Atlas plunges two fingers into my pussy, stealing the words from my lips. "Fuck," I moan, turning my gaze to the ceiling so he can't see the pleasure in my eyes. I expect him to drop his mouth back to my clit, so when his lips press against the inside of my thigh, I peer down at him—right before his fangs sink into the delicate skin there.

I cry out, a mixture of pleasure and pain spiking through me as Atlas drinks deeply. My clit throbs in response, and he pulses his fingers inside me, curling them at just the right spot. I reach under my shirt, hiking it up as my hands slide under my bra, and roll my nipples between my fingers. My breaths come in little gasps, my cheeks hot as I race toward release. Pressure builds low in my belly, and the sensation of Atlas taking my blood while pushing his fingers deep inside me sends me over the edge. The walls of my pussy clench around his fingers, soaking them with my release as he continues pumping them in and out while I ride the orgasm to completion, basking in the delicious aftershocks of my climax.

I shiver when he pulls his fingers—and fangs—out of me. He seals the puncture marks with a quick drag of his tongue along my skin and crawls over me, the bulge in his pants stealing my attention immediately.

"You," I say rather breathlessly, "are wearing entirely too much clothing."

His eyes glimmer with a dangerous mix of lust and hunger as he tilts his head to the side. "Is that right?"

My eyes flick to his erection, and I press my lips together against a smile. "Well, yeah. If you want to do something about that."

He captures my chin and licks his lips. "What I *want* is to fuck that smart mouth of yours."

I stare at him, my eyes widening at his words. I want to look away, to hide the flush of my cheeks. I press my lips together as he watches me.

"Nothing to say now?" he taunts, tugging his shirt off in one fluid motion, dropping it on the floor.

"I've got plenty," I say, reaching for the button on his

pants, "but I was raised to know that talking with a mouthful is rude." Of course, my mouth isn't full of anything yet, but I don't know what else to say. Because I'm pretty fucking far out of my element with Atlas.

He laughs, the deep sound filling the room as he pulls back and stands, unzipping his pants and tugging them along with his boxers to his ankles. His cock, now free of its confinement, springs to attention, and I can't pull my eyes away. I still can't believe that thing fits inside me. It makes me shiver at the memory of how it felt, my pussy clenching around it. *I want it again.*

"Come here," Altas beckons me, his voice thick with arousal, and offers me a hand. When I take it, he pulls me up so I'm sitting at the end of his bed, putting me at eye level with his cock.

Something takes hold of me, and I move without hesitation, reaching for him. I wrap my fingers around the base of his thick length, slowly pumping and alternating pressure.

He hisses out a sharp breath, and my lips curl into a satisfied grin. I quite literally have him in the palm of my hand, and as badly as I want his cock buried inside me, I'm not going to rush this moment. Because right now, *I'm* in control. *He's* going to take what *I* give him.

I lean forward as moisture beads at the tip of his cock and lightly flick my tongue along it to capture the saltiness there as I continue moving my hand up and down his shaft.

"Fuck," he breathes, his hand gripping my shoulder firmly but not to a painful degree.

Slowly, I wrap my lips around him, pushing down and taking him into my mouth, my tongue gliding along the underside of his cock. His grip on my shoulder tightens, and I close my eyes, focusing on keeping my throat relaxed so I can take more of him. He moves his hand from my shoulder to the back of my neck, guiding himself in further until he hits the back of my throat. I will my gag reflex not to kick in, my pulse pounding beneath my skin. Finally, he lets up and I pull back slowly, sucking and licking as I start bobbing up and down, taking as much of him as I can. His hand stays wrapped around the back of my neck, but he isn't applying any pressure; I'm still controlling this.

He exhales a harsh, short breath, and I reach down and take his balls in my hands, massaging them as I increase the pressure of my lips around his shaft.

"Calla," he grounds out, and I'm not sure if my name on his lips is a curse or a prayer. Perhaps it's both. "Slow down, or I'm going to come in your mouth in a minute."

My stomach swirls with warmth, the throbbing between my legs growing more intense knowing how much my ministrations are affecting him. I've never been the biggest fan of performing oral, but the thought of driving Atlas to release with my mouth spurs me on, and I move quicker instead of slowing down.

Atlas's grip on my neck tightens. "Fuck, Calla," he growls.

I moan, my lips vibrating against his cock, sucking harder as I continue working his balls. They tighten in my hands, which is my only warning before he groans deeply, shooting his release against the back of my throat. I force myself to swallow as much as I can, but some spills out the side of my mouth, rolling down my chin. Atlas pulls me off his cock and uses his thumb to clean his release off my face. He cups my cheek, dipping his head to kiss me with enough intensity to make me grab him and pull him on top of me. He moves at an inhuman speed, somehow maneuvering us so he's lying under me and I'm straddling his waist, his cock pressing against my back.

I steady myself on top of him, my palms flat against his chest. He grips my hips, and I push my ass against his cock, looking down at him with a grin. His eyes devour me and a muscle ticks in his jaw.

I arch a brow at him. "What?"

He fingers the hem of my shirt. "Now who's wearing too much clothing?"

Offering a short laugh, I pull my shirt off over my head, tossing it to the side of the bed, leaving me in nothing but my bra.

Atlas's fingers skim up my sides, making me shiver, then he reaches behind me and unclasps my bra, pulling it off and exposing my breasts to his hungry gaze.

At that moment, my body floods with heat under his scrutiny. I'm left completely bared to him, and it's making my heart pound in my chest. I turn my face away, suddenly feeling wickedly self-conscious. Atlas has been around for over a century; I can't be anything special. My thoughts veer into dangerous territory, and I'm thinking about all the women he must've been with before me. Surely some of them were far more experienced than I am, and—

"Calla." Atlas's voice pulls me back, but I still can't bring myself to meet his gaze. His hands are back on my hips, his thumbs rubbing slow circles against my skin. "What's going on in that head of yours?" he asks. "Already regretting this?"

My eyes widen. Of all the things he could say, that was the least of what I was expecting. "No."

"Then look at me."

I catch my bottom lip between my teeth, peering down at him, focusing on the dark stubble covering his chin.

He says my name again, and I finally lift my eyes to his, my heart in my throat.

"You are the most stunning creature I've laid eyes on," he murmurs, reaching up to tuck my hair behind my ear. "There is nothing on this earth that will keep me from you." His gaze darkens as his hand returns to my hip and gives it a squeeze. "Wherever you are, I will find you."

Every word in my vocabulary vanishes. Gone. *Poof.* I have no idea what led Atlas to say those words to me, but something in my chest is clinging to them.

Maybe vampires *can* read minds. That, or my face gave my thoughts of insecurity away more than I'd like to consider.

I lean down until my chest is pressed against his and my fingers are in his hair, then brush my lips over his. "I want you inside me," I murmur against his lips.

He nips my bottom lip, his hands reaching around to cup my ass and grind me against his cock. "So take it."

My heart lurches and feels as if it's lodged in my throat. "What?"

Atlas smirks. "Ride me, Calla."

I blush hotly, chewing the inside of my cheek. "Right."

"Lift your hips," he instructs in a deep voice.

I do as he says, and he shifts under me, positioning the head of his cock so it lines up with my entrance. All I have to do is lower myself onto him. He rubs along my slit, coaxing me to push down, and I hold my breath as I sink onto him one inch at a time.

"Breathe," he says, his eyes glimmering with amusement.

I force a breath in and out, lowering the rest of the way so I'm seated on him. I've never been this full before. He feels so much deeper than when he took me against the tree.

Holy hell, this is fucking amazing.

I lift my hips, moving up his shaft before dropping back down a little faster this time, eliciting a moan from my lips.

Atlas closes his eyes, holding my hips, but letting me lead as I balance myself on top of him, alternating my pace here and there, making him groan beneath me.

"That's it," he encourages, reaching between us to play with my clit as I continue to ride his cock.

I tip my head back, closing my eyes as our heavy breathing fills the room. I moan, not even making an effort to be quiet, and Atlas lifts his hips to thrust into me, stealing my breath.

"Yes," I pant, moving quicker still, and my breasts bounce with each thrust.

"Fuck," Atlas groans. "Look at me. I want to watch you take my cock, riding me until you come."

My eyes fly open, meeting his liquid silver gaze as I drop onto his cock over and over, crying out when my pussy walls tighten. My muscles squeeze his cock as his fingers work my clit until I see fucking stars. He thrusts into me hard and fast, his climax quickly following mine, and he announces his release with a deep grunt before pulling me down onto him and sealing his mouth over mine. His lips dominate me as he continues thrusting his hips, and I ride the aftershocks of my orgasm, kissing him back with fervor.

He wraps his arms around me, rolling us so we're lying on our sides facing each other, and pulls out of me without breaking the kiss. I shiver as his cock brushes my clit and slide my fingers into his hair again, pulling him closer to me.

We break apart to breathe, and I trace the lines of his chest with a single finger as he presses his lips to my forehead. It's the sweetest thing he's ever done, and it makes my chest tighten, reminding me that he's leaving in the morning.

"I don't want you to go," I whisper too low for any human to pick up on it.

But Atlas isn't human.

His soft exhale stirs the hair at my temple. "Everything is going to be fine," he says in a level tone.

"You don't know that." I try to pull away, but he holds me against him.

"Let's not talk about it. There's nothing to be said or done. I'm going to the summit. End of story."

"Fine," I mumble, closing my eyes. It's not an argument I want to get into, nor do I have the energy for, especially considering I won't win. Instead of pushing it, I shift closer, resting my head against his chest, and let myself relax enough to drift off, listening to the steady beat of Atlas's heart.

I guess he has one after all.

Atlas is gone before any of us wake the next morning. Lex is still passed out when I pry my eyes open and immediately smell the sweet aroma of cooking coming from the kitchen. There's also a lingering scent of coffee, which is what truly hauls my ass out of the rickety bed. I don't bother putting on a shirt, walking down the creaky floored hallway in nothing but my boxers. I round the corner into the kitchen and lean against the wall, my lips curling into a faint smile as I watch Calla stirring pancake batter in a stainless steel mixing bowl. She drops a handful of chocolate chips into the batter and another handful into her mouth.

She's so fucking sexy, I can't take my eyes off her. I want to sneak up behind her and wrap my arms around her, pressing her against me. More than that, the desire to hoist her onto the counter and bury my head between her thighs sends a rush of heat straight to my cock.

Setting the bowl on the counter, she walks over to the stove and flips the pancakes already cooking in the pan, humming softly under her breath before turning toward the fridge. Her eyes land on me, and she yelps, her hand smacking against her chest in surprise.

"What the hell, Kade?" she grumbles, her heart still racing, and I certainly don't miss the way her eyes linger on my bare chest.

I chuckle softly, pushing away from the wall and walking closer to her. "Good morning to you too."

She rolls her eyes, and I half expect her to flip me off, but she just opens the fridge and proceeds to ignore me. Huh. Guess she wasn't so overtaken by lust at the sight of my abs to not get annoyed with me for sneaking up on her.

"You should be in a better mood after last night," I say, my voice laced with amusement. We all heard what she and Atlas got up to, and it took every ounce of self-control I have not to invite myself. Gabriel insisted that we leave the two of them alone—that they both needed it. Which, fine, whatever. But damn. I've only experienced the mastery that is Atlas York in bed on a handful of occasions. The tinge of jealousy was annoying as fuck.

"I'm fine," she says, slamming the fridge door shut and setting the block of butter on the counter.

I hold my hands up in mock defense. "Easy. I'm only messing with you."

"Yeah, well, for once, could you just not?"

The grin falls from my lips. "Hey." I close the distance between us and turn her around to face me. "What's going on?"

Her jaw clenches, her eyes flicking between mine. "Nothing," she says flatly.

I hold her still when she tries to pull away. "Calla."

"Kade," she levels in a tight voice.

I sigh. "I'm worried about him too, but Atlas can take care of himself."

She blinks, her hard expression softening as her brows

knit. I can tell she's clinging to a facade of strength, and while I admire the hell out of that, part of me wants her to know she doesn't have to. That we'll be strong *for* her.

"I know," she says. "I still think we should've gone with him."

I move my hand off her shoulder and brush my knuckles across her cheek. "He'll be back and annoying the hell out of you before you know it."

Calla lets out a heavy sigh. "Yeah, all right." Her eyes flick between mine. "I'm worried about you too, you know."

"I'm fine," I say automatically, ignoring the pressure in my chest. I don't want Calla to worry about me, to see the darkness swirling inside me, or the suffocating anxiety I experience when my thoughts drift to my sister.

"I don't believe you," she whispers.

I force a smile. "Okay. Then I *will* be fine."

Calla sighs, clearly recognizing that she's not going to get much more out of me. "You hungry?" she asks.

I tap the tip of her nose. "Sure. I'll go wake the others."

She nods, turning back to the stove to flip the cooked pancakes onto a plate before pouring more batter into the frying pan. "Gabriel's asleep on the couch."

I stop in the living room, nudging the couch cushion with my foot until Gabriel rouses, squinting at me. "Wakey, wakey," I say in a singsong voice.

He blinks his eyes open and sits up, running his fingers through his copper hair. "He's gone."

I nod. "Not sure when he left, but I'm sure he'll check in when he can."

Gabriel returns my nod and stands, shuffling into the kitchen, no doubt to the coffee machine.

I return to the bedroom and grab my pillow, proceeding to smack Lex in the face with it. "Get up."

"Fuck off," he grumbles, rolling onto his stomach and covering his head with the pillow.

"Calla's making breakfast for everyone. Don't be an asshole. Come eat with us."

His responding laugh is muffled by another pillow. "Calla doesn't cook."

"She bakes, though. I think pancakes are essentially baking. She mixed water and some powdered shit." I shrug, tugging the sheets off him and exposing his bare ass. I snicker. "Get up, put on some pants, and come eat."

He groans, turning back over. "In that order?"

My eyes flick to his impressive erection, and I smirk. "Preferably."

With that, I quickly pull on a pair of black joggers and walk back to the kitchen, where Gabriel is leaning against the counter nursing a cup of coffee while he chats with Calla about a French toast recipe he wants to show her when we have a better functioning kitchen.

Once we're all squeezed around the dining table stuffing our faces with pancakes, Gabriel announces that Atlas made it to New York. If I should feel better about that, I don't. Atlas's parents are some of the most wicked vampires in existence. They have zero regard for human life and care only for the preservation of their kind. I have no fucking clue how Atlas can stand them; they scare the absolute shit out of me.

"What happens now?" Calla asks, taking a sip of orange juice. Her pulse is ticking unevenly and her brows are knit.

"We'll head to the new place once Atlas is finished at the summit. It'll depend on what information he brings back what we do after that."

She nods, then sighs softly before pushing her plate away, half-eaten. "I'm, uh, going to get cleaned up." She doesn't wait for any of us to respond before she stands and carries her dishes into the kitchen. Her footsteps grow softer as she walks down the hall toward the bathroom.

My chair scrapes across the floor as I stand, leaving my plate to follow her. I'm not sure what makes me do it, but I need to check on her.

The bathroom door isn't completely closed, so I knock once and slowly push it open enough to slip inside, then shut it behind me. The bathroom is the only part of the house that seems to be newly renovated. With his and hers sinks and a massive claw-foot tub, it looks as if the previous owners started in this room and never had a chance to finish the rest of the house.

Calla is bent over, turning on the water to fill the tub. She stands, turning to face me, and says, "What are you doing?" Her voice is small, tired.

"I wanted to make sure you're okay," I tell her, leaning against the wall beside the door.

She grabs a bottle of bubble bath from the vanity and squirts some under the water. "I'm as okay as any of us can be at this point, Kade."

"That's a copout answer."

"Fine." She sets the bottle back on the vanity and crosses her arms over her chest. "Are *you* okay? With everything going on, you haven't had a chance to deal with what happened with your sister."

So she's going to try and get me to talk again. Arching a brow at her, I say, "I came to check on you, and you're asking how I am?"

Her arms fall to her sides, and she leans against the vanity, flicking a glance toward the tub to check the water level before looking at me again. "Um, yeah. Are you going to tell me?"

I blow out a heavy breath. "Honestly, I have no idea what to do. Or if there's anything I *should* do, for that matter. I don't know what Meredith's plan is, or why she seems to be working with the hunters. At this point, she's the enemy. And yeah, that really fucking sucks." I shove my hands into the pockets of my joggers to hide the way they're shaking. I'd like to believe I've done well hiding how much my sister's sudden appearance has affected me. But the more I think about it, the more it doesn't make sense. I'm so confused, and the only one who holds the answers that will resolve that confusion is my sister.

Calla frowns. "I'm really sorry, Kade. I wish there was something I could do to make it easier for you." She walks closer, stopping an arms' reach away. "You can talk to me about her, you know. Anytime. I'm a good listener."

I offer her a wry grin. "Thanks. I've also been known to be a good listener."

"I'm pretty much at a loss," she admits. "These days, I have no idea what's happening or *going* to happen. There's a new threat every day, and despite that, I find myself worrying about school of all things, which is ridiculous in comparison to the other shit we're facing, I am fully aware of that. And the more I think about the aforementioned shit, the bigger this pit in my stomach grows, because I am scared—so fucking scared of what's going to happen and the possibility that I might lose one of you…" Her voice trails off and her eyes widen; she's surprised by her own words.

*She's worried about losing us.*

My chest is oddly tight, and I have the urge to wrap her in my arms and never let go, never let her think that anything or anyone could get in the way or threaten what we have.

Calla sighs and finally says, "But I kinda came in here to get *away* from the talking."

I nod slowly, wanting to assure her that I won't push it. "We don't have to talk." I dip my face so my lips are at her ear. "I'm also very good at *not* talking."

The hitch in her breath is all I need. I pull my hands out of my pockets and grab her around the waist, pulling her against me.

"Kade," she breathes, and the sound of my name on her lips goes right to my cock.

"Tell me what you need," I say, trailing my mouth along her jaw as she presses her palms against my bare chest.

She trails her fingers upward as she leans up on her tiptoes and connects them at the back of my neck, turning her face so my mouth lands on hers. She kisses me slowly at first—until I press my lower half into her, then she moans into my mouth, deepening the kiss as she grips the back of my hair.

I return her kiss, guiding us toward the tub, where the water is at the perfect level. I manage to reach over and turn it off without breaking the kiss. I nip her bottom lip, grazing my tongue along it, and her pulse kicks up.

She leans back and grabs the hem of her shirt, quickly tugging it off, revealing her breasts. Her nipples are pebbled, and I lick my lips, wanting nothing more than to drop my mouth to her skin and devour them.

Calla places a finger under my chin, tilting my head up to return my gaze to her face to find her soft brown eyes filled with desire, with need—and I am more than happy to oblige.

I give her a chaste kiss before curling my fingers into the waistband of her pants, crouching as I tug them down to her ankles. Her hand rests on my shoulder as she steps out of them, kicking them into a pile with her shirt. When I straighten, her cheeks are flushed, and I reach for her, tucking her hair behind her ear. I take her hand, guiding her to the tub, and she steps in, lowering herself under the bubbles as steam fills the room, fogging the mirrors and filling the space with a calming haze of eucalyptus and mint.

Stepping out of my pants and boxers, I get into the tub.

Calla slides forward, so I lower myself behind her and pull her back against my chest. I move her hair over one shoulder and press my lips to the other, kissing toward her neck, where I suck gently, swirling my tongue against her warm skin.

Calla sighs, tipping her head back against my shoulder. "Touch me," she says in a voice so low any human would miss it.

My lips curl into a grin against her neck. "I *am* touching you."

She lets out a little impatient noise, her hands gliding along my thighs beneath the water. "You know that's not what I mean."

"Hmm…" I lift my hands to her shoulders, massaging them with slow, deep movements. "I think you're going to need to be more specific, Calla."

She inhales slowly. "You're such an ass," she mutters, but her voice is gentle, soft with relaxation.

I chuckle. "You like it."

Calla reaches back and grabs my hands, pulling them over her shoulders and down her chest to her breasts. "Do I need to tell you what to do with these?" she taunts.

My cock twitches at her tone, and I cup her breasts, my fingers working her nipples into stiff pebbles. "I think I can manage."

She sucks in a breath, turning her head and pressing her lips to my collarbone, then my jaw before her lips find mine, and she moans against them.

"I want to taste you," I murmur, nipping her lower lip as my gums throb, my fangs threatening to break through them.

She breaks the kiss, her heart pounding in her chest. "If you want my blood," she says in a shallow voice, "put your hand between my legs and make me come."

It takes every ounce of my self-control not to drive my

cock into her from behind. I settle for trailing my hand down her stomach until my fingers disappear under the bubbles and water to brush the inside of her thigh. My lips find her neck, and I kiss her there, running my finger along her folds. Satisfaction floods through me when her breathing hitches, and she spreads her legs open for me. "That's my girl," I murmur, my lips tracing the shell of her ear, making her squirm. I dip a finger past her folds and apply a bit of pressure to her clit, moving my thumb over it in a circular motion.

"More," she demands, breathing heavily, and I am more than happy to oblige.

I slide my finger inside her pussy, curling it before pulling out, then add a second finger, pushing back in to my knuckles.

She bites her lip, her head bent back against my chest and her eyes closed. "Yes."

"You like that?" I drag my tongue along her neck, and she pushes her ass against my dick. "Message received," I say, my lips dancing across the delicate skin below her ear as my fingers pump in and out of her soaked pussy. Her thighs shake and her heels slam into the bottom of the tub.

"Don't stop," she pants, pushing against my fingers, riding them.

"Are you close?" I whisper lowly in her ear.

She sucks in a shallow breath. "Y-yes. Holy shit."

Heat floods through me, and if my dick wasn't rock solid before, it sure as fuck is now. "I want to feel you clench around my fingers as I sink my fangs into your throat."

"Yes," she nearly whimpers, tilting her head and baring her neck to me. "Please."

Her soft words have my fangs slicing through my gums in an instant, and I press my thumb against her clit, circling it hard and fast as I fuck her with my fingers and sink my fangs into her neck. Her sweet, hot blood explodes on my tongue, and I close my eyes, drinking deeply. My cock twitches with need as her blood warms my stomach, and I increase my thrusts into her.

"*Kade*," she cries out in a high-pitched voice, coming around my fingers, squeezing them as she grinds against me, reveling in the pleasure of her climax.

My fingers continue pumping as her legs shake and her breaths come in shallow pants while she rides the after-shocks of her orgasm, her release coating my fingers and seeping into the tub.

When my need to bury my cock deep inside her over-powers my desire for her blood, I pull back, healing my bite, and maneuver us in a blur of motion, spilling a bit of water on the bathroom tile.

"What are you doing?" she asks with a short laugh, still catching her breath.

I reach under the water and lift her leg to the ledge of the tub. "Hold it there," I tell her, fisting my cock in my hand, pumping my hand along its length a few times before lining it up with her entrance. I tease her with the thick head, making her moan as I drag it along her slit, dipping in inch by inch until my full length is buried in her throbbing heat. "Fuck," I hiss out through my teeth. "You feel so good."

"This angle doesn't," she grumbles.

Fair enough. She's on her side with her leg up and her ass pressed against the back of the tub.

"Allow me to fix that." I grab her around the waist and stand while remaining mostly inside her. I manage to get us out of the tub and plant her sweet ass on the vanity. I roll my hips, pushing all the way into her, and she grabs my shoulder, biting her lip to quiet the sound of her moan, with her eyes closed and her head tipped back against the steam-covered mirror.

I pick up the pace and slide my hand up her stomach, between her breasts and past her collarbone until my fingers wrap around her throat. I don't apply pressure, I just hold her to the mirror, my cock hardening inside her at the rapid beat of her pulse against my fingers. My balls tighten, and I groan, pumping hard and fast as tension builds quickly. I reach between us with my other hand and find her clit, flicking it once, twice, three times, making her gasp each time, then rub two fingers over it in a slow, circular motion.

She bites her lip so hard, the smell of her blood hits my senses, and I slam into her.

"Don't hold back," I order. "I want to hear every sound you make as I ravish you."

Her responding exhale is uneven, and when my cock hits a particularly sensitive spot deep inside her, the lovely sound of her moans fill the warm, hazy room.

"Good girl." I reward her by quickening my thrusts, pulsing my fingers around her clit.

"Fuck, I'm going to—"

"Come," I say in a velvet-smooth voice, thrusting so hard her ass slides back on the vanity. "Come for me, Calla."

"Mmm... *ohmygod*, yessss," she cries out, gripping my shoulders so hard, her fingernails bite into my skin. I barely feel it. She could stake me in the fucking heart right now, and I wouldn't give a damn. Not with her wrapped around my cock.

"That's it," I encourage her, driving into her over and over as my own orgasm builds. Her walls squeeze me perfectly, throbbing and clenching around me, and I groan loudly, spurting my release inside her as I come. "Fuck," I growl, tugging her to me and slamming my lips against hers, holding my cock still in her heat.

Our lips move together as if we've been together for over a century. As if our bodies know each other on a molecular level. Which, in a sense, I suppose they do. Blood oath and all.

The idea makes my chest tighten, and I break the kiss. The thought of that damn oath having any part of what we just did makes me feel oddly sick to my stomach.

"You know," she says, resting her forehead against my chest, catching her breath. "We started off in the tub, but I feel dirtier than ever." She plants soft kisses across my chest, and I can't help but chuckle, forcing myself to shove away any thoughts of what brought us together.

I catch her chin, tilting her face up to meet my gaze as I slowly slide out of her. "If you're waiting for an apology, you're not getting one," I tease.

Calla arches a brow at me, her cheeks flushed a lovely shade of pink. "For that?" She laughs. "Hardly."

Offering a grin, I kiss her forehead and grab a towel from the shelf next to the vanity before lifting her off it and wrapping her up.

She holds the front of the towel and walks toward the bathroom door, glancing back at me over her shoulder. "Good talk." She winks at me, and my grin widens.

I take another towel and tie it around my waist, following her out of the bathroom. She walks down the hall to one bedroom, while I go to the other, tugging on a fresh T-shirt and dark jeans. I'm doing up the buckle on my belt when my phone chimes from the wicker—yes, *wicker*—table beside the bed. I snatch it up, expecting an update from Atlas, and the phone nearly slips from my fingers when my eyes land on the message.

*We need to talk, brother.*

So she knows I'm alive, that her ambush before the hunter attack didn't kill me.

And she has my phone number.

My stomach plummets, and I sink onto the end of the

bed, gripping the phone in my hand, and my fingers glide over the keyboard.

*Pass. Last time we hung out, you tried to kill me.*

Her response comes moments later.

*Your humor hasn't changed, K. And I didn't try to kill you. If I'd wanted you dead, you wouldn't be alive.*

I despise the way my fingers shake as they hover over the keys.

*You know, that's not very comforting. What do you want to meet for?*

Once I hit send, I force my legs to stand and walk to the living room, where Gabriel is reading something on his phone and Lex is lounging on the couch, drinking from a blood bag as if it's a juice box.

Lex catches the look on my face and arches a questioning brow at me.

"We may have a problem."

Gabriel looks up from his phone. "What's going on?"

"Meredith wants me to meet her."

"Yeah, no," Lex says. "Sister or not, the little psycho stabbed you."

"Lex," Gabriel warns.

I frown, though I understand where he's coming from. If someone from his past showed up and skewered him, I wouldn't be too keen on him meeting up with them a second time.

"What does she want?" Gabriel asks.

My gaze drops to my phone as it vibrates with another message from Meredith.

*I owe you an explanation.*

Lex scowls when I read the text aloud. "No fucking kidding."

Gabriel pinches the bridge of his nose, sighing. "Do you want to go?"

My stomach twists. Part of me feels I need to, to hear what she has to say, but the last thing any of us need right now is another ambush. "I... I think so."

He offers a curt nod. "We should at least wait until Atlas is back. We can go with you and make sure she doesn't try to pull anything a second time."

Lex tosses the empty blood bag on the coffee table. "I want proof it isn't a trap."

I press my lips together and type a response to my sister.

My sister.

Fuck. I still can't wrap my head around her being alive—and like me. I have so many questions, but maybe with this meeting, I'll finally get some answers.

*Say I agree to meet you. How can I be sure it's not a trap? I'm sure it comes as no surprise that I don't trust you.*

I lean against the armrest of the couch after I send my reply and wait.

*That's fair. But you should take into consideration that I didn't tell the hunters about the human consort you have.*

I bark out a bitter laugh. She thinks Calla is our consort. Vampires have been known to keep humans around to feed on or complete household tasks, but that has absolutely nothing to do with the reason Calla is with us.

I often pretend the blood oath doesn't have anything to do with it either, but that's beside the point.

"She's making jokes now?" Lex says, his sharp silver eyes narrowed on me, though I know his anger is not directed *at* me.

"You could say that. She thinks Calla is our consort."

Lex's expression softens, and he snorts out a laugh. "Right."

I rub my hand down my face, then reply with, *I don't see what that has to do with anything. And why should I believe anything you say to me now?*

A minute goes by. Then two. Five minutes later, she still hasn't responded.

Finally, after what feels like the longest fifteen minutes of my eternal existence, my phone buzzes with her reply.

*I've never lied to you before, have I? Being a vampire doesn't change who you are as a person. I'm no liar, Kade.*

With a sigh, I write back and tell her we'll meet on Friday at a location to be determined once I know where we'll be and knowing Atlas will be with us again in case I need backup. That also gives me a few days to prepare myself for whatever I'm walking into with her.

This meeting has the potential to be a complete disaster. Despite that, there's a tiny, annoying-as-fuck spark of hope in my chest. And I can't help but cling to it.

❧ 12 ❧

## CALLA

"**H**is car just pulled in."

My stomach does a little flip, but I force myself to stay on the couch instead of running outside and launching myself at him.

Atlas was gone for two days. We didn't hear much out of New York during that time, save for a couple of quick texts from him assuring us he was fine, bored if anything, and that he'd fill us in when he got back.

Gabriel gets up and walks to the front door. I catch sight of Atlas through the window in the living room, throwing his duffle bag over his shoulder and walking toward the house, and my breath gets caught in my throat. The pull in my chest and the pounding of my heart isn't something I was expecting.

Lex and Kade disappeared after breakfast to pack what few things we have, but they both walk into the living room and drop into the chairs on either side of the unlit fireplace.

The front door opens and the sound of hushed voices reaches me. My throat goes dry, and I swallow hard, my eyes snapping to the doorway when Atlas steps into the room.

He's dressed in all black—combat boots, jeans, V-neck, and a leather jacket. His hair is a mess from the wind and his under eyes are shadowed with sleepless nights.

I'm off the couch, closing the distance between us before I fully come to terms with what I'm doing. Between one moment and the next, I launch myself at him, wrapping my arms around his neck and burying my face in his chest. He stumbles back half a step. Atlas York *stumbles*. Clearly he's as taken by surprise at my greeting as I am. But then his arms come around me—one snakes around my waist and the other slides into my hair, cradling my head against his chest.

I inhale deeply, closing my eyes as his scent envelops me, settling my racing heart. I suppose there was a part of me that was worried about him and I didn't realize how deep that worry ran until I saw him.

"Aww, I love it when Mom and Dad get along." Kade's voice bursts my bubble of momentary calm, and I move away from Atlas, shooting Kade a glare over my shoulder.

When my eyes flit back to Atlas, my chest tightens. He looks like shit. I mean, he's still easily one of the most attractive men—scratch that, *people*—I've ever seen, but his face is a canvas of darkness. His jaw is set tight; he's on high-alert now, but he's also exhausted.

He drops his chin, glancing down at me. "Don't look at me like that," he says in a low voice. "I'm fine."

I shake my head. "Liar."

His lips twitch. "I'll live, then."

Crossing my arms, I narrow my eyes at him. "You—"

"He just needs to feed," Lex interjects from across the living room. "What, they didn't feed you in New York?"

Atlas leans against the door frame as Gabriel shifts around him, walking to the couch and dropping onto it. "Nothing I wanted."

My brows knit in confusion. "You didn't feed at all while you were there?"

"I don't particularly like the way they choose to feed and I didn't have time to find my own means."

Nervously, I ask, "What does that mean?"

"It doesn't matter," he says with a tone of finality.

I want to push, but if I've learned anything being with these guys it's to pick my battles, so I nod. And then I grab his wrist and pull him down the hall toward the bedroom I've been sleeping in. Once we're inside, I close the door and let go of his wrist, moving the hair away from my neck.

He sighs. "Calla—"

"Take what you need."

"It's not your responsibility to ensure I have blood to drink." He steps closer, lowering his voice. "You are not our feeder."

*You're far more than that.*

He doesn't say it, but with the way he's looking at me, the storm of desire in his eyes, he doesn't have to.

"I don't care," I say, and my voice comes out quieter than I intended. I swallow, then add, "I want to make you feel better. What's wrong with that?"

His eyes flick between mine, and he lifts his hand to my face, his fingers skimming over my cheek so softly I barely feel it. "I haven't fed in a few days, and after the days I've had… I could hurt you."

I reach for the dagger at my thigh, patting it where it sits securely in its guard. "I can defend myself," I offer, my pulse ticking faster.

Atlas presses his lips into a thin line. "Do you truly believe that once I get my fangs in your neck you could fight me off if I lose control?"

"No," I say firmly. I've been training, yes, but I'm not naive enough to believe I could fight off a vampire once they sink their fangs into me. "I don't think you'll lose control."

"Then you are too trusting."

I shrug. "I never said I trusted you."

"Didn't you?" he questions with a subtle tilt of his head. "You're offering yourself to me knowing full well you won't be able to defend yourself if things go wrong. You're trusting that things won't go wrong. That I have control enough over the monster in me that wants to tear into your carotid artery and devour your blood."

Without missing a beat, I say dryly, "And they say romance is dead."

He exhales a short laugh, shaking his head. "Calla—"

"God, Atlas," I cut him off. "Quit being such a martyr. Do you really think the three other vampires in this house would sit by and let you suck me dry?"

He lets out a heavy sigh before his dark gaze falls on my neck, making my throat go dry. I instinctively step back, then remind myself that I wanted to do this. His silver gaze slams into me a moment before he strikes, moving at a preternatural speed. His arm circles my waist, pulling me flush against his chest as his other hand cradles the side of my head. A low growl rumbles through him, and I close my eyes, tilting my head to the side seconds before his fangs sink into my neck, stealing my breath. There's a brief moment of white-hot, searing pain, but then it's gone, replaced by warmth and pleasure.

Atlas drinks deeply, and I lean into him, giving myself over to the endorphins rushing through me. I gasp softly when his erection presses against the throbbing between my legs. Heat gathers low in my belly, and my breasts tingle with the desire to be touched. I press my lips together to keep from moaning and cling to him, my head starting to spin.

A minute later, he pulls back, dragging his tongue over

the puncture marks on my neck. He keeps his arm around me, and I sway into his chest.

"Calla, open your eyes for me."

"Hmm…" I try to pry them open, but they're too heavy. I just want to sleep and for him to keep holding me. My skin tingles everywhere he touches, and I feel as if I'm floating on a cloud of warmth.

He grasps my chin, tilting my head up. "Don't make me feed you my blood."

Right now, that doesn't sound as awful as it usually does. In fact, the thought only makes the heat between my legs intensify.

A rumble of laughter vibrates through his chest. "Yeah, that's what I thought. Come on. You need to eat something."

We start walking toward the living room, and by *we* and *walking*, I mean, Atlas practically carries me there with how much I'm leaning on him just to stay upright.

I've never felt so equally weak and aroused before. It's an odd thing.

Atlas guides me to the couch, and Gabriel is there a second later, setting a plate with a sandwich and glass of orange juice on the coffee table in front of me.

I smile at him as I reach for the glass, my hand shaking a little. "Thanks."

Four sets of silver eyes are honed on me while I inhale the sandwich, washing it down with the juice. With food in my system, I gain back some of my strength and don't feel as if I'm going to pass out at any second, which is nice.

Gabriel sits next to me, while Atlas leans against the mantle between Kade and Lex.

I turn my gaze to Atlas. "Are you going to fill us in on what went down in New York?"

A muscle in his jaw ticks, but he nods. "I don't agree with what they've decided to do, but I was outvoted by a lot," he prefaces before sighing. "Many of the older born vampires want to take out the hunters, starting with the headquarters in Washington using the information I've gathered from being inside Ellis Industries. I have names and addresses of most of the D.C. hunters... and I provided that information during the summit."

"Shit," Lex mutters, rubbing his jaw.

Gabriel and Kade remain silent, and the food in my stomach suddenly feels like concrete.

I clench my jaw against the nausea rippling through me and swallow past the bile rising in my throat. "What does that mean?" I force the words out, willing my stomach to settle.

Atlas's expression remains impassive. "There has been an attack planned. Its goal is to wipe out as many of the hunters as possible in one night. It's happening in three days. We needed time to spread the word to as many vampires as possible and get them on board for the attack. The idea is to attack every place we can simultaneously so there's little chance of a real fight."

Tears prick my eyes and my mouth fills with saliva as my stomach churns more violently. If the vampires attack Scott Ellis, Brighton is in just as much danger as he is. And as conflicted as I am over finding out that Scott basically runs the hunters, he has always been kind to me since Bri and I became friends years ago. The thought of their family home being attacked by vicious, vengeful vampires makes my head spin so fast my vision blurs.

My chest fills with pressure and my hand flies to my mouth. I'm off the couch in a rush. Gabriel reaches for me, but I pull back and run to the bathroom. I drop to the floor and barely manage to get the lid of the toilet up before I empty my stomach into the bowl. Tears roll down my cheeks, and I jump when a hand touches my shoulder.

Wiping my mouth with the back of my hand, I turn my head enough to see Atlas crouching behind me. I blink at him in surprise; he's the last one I would've guessed would come after me.

Atlas moves his hand from my shoulder and collects my hair, pulling it away from my face just in time for me to turn back to the toilet and heave until my throat is dry and my head is pounding. He rubs my back until I stop vomiting, then stands and walks over to the vanity, filling a glass with water as I sink onto the floor, leaning against the wall and struggling to breathe. Each breath is a short, shallow gasp; it feels as if someone is standing on my chest, crushing my lungs, and darkness dances along the edge of my vision.

Atlas appears in front of me again, crouching and bringing the glass to my lips. He helps me drink a little, but I immediately start coughing, which doesn't help with the hyperventilating I'm already doing.

He sets the glass on the floor beside me, holding my gaze. "You need to breathe, Calla."

*I'm fucking trying*, I want to say, but the words… I can't make them form, so I just shake my head, continuing to fight for every breath.

His eyes soften a fraction, and I think I see concern in them. His hands land on my cheeks, soft but firm, and he snares my gaze. The moment his glamour falls over me, the tightness in my chest eases.

"Breathe," he murmurs.

I try to pull in a breath and find I can. It's a bit stunted, but my lungs fill.

"Good. Now let it out slowly."

I close my eyes to focus, letting the air out through my mouth.

His glamour holds despite our eyes no longer being

locked; his fingers graze my cheeks, holding the connection. "Again."

We sit on the floor as I regain the ability to breathe on my own. Eventually he releases me and we end up sitting next to each other against the wall.

"I understand your concern about what came of the summit," he says in a level voice. "This isn't something I wanted." He turns his head to look at me. "I give you my word I will make sure Brighton is safe. She will not be harmed."

I bite my bottom lip to keep it from trembling. Brighton doesn't deserve to be anywhere near this. She also doesn't deserve to lose her father, but that—asking Atlas to spare the life of Scott Ellis—isn't going to happen. I'm grateful he at least cares enough about me to ensure Brighton will be okay, but that is going to leave me having to help my best friend through losing one of her parents.

I'm unsettled at how strangely calm Atlas is over this whole situation. It's mass murder. Granted the humans they'll be going after have killed countless vampires, it doesn't change the facts. Not to mention, these are the same people who attacked all of us at the house, so it's a little hard not to be twisted up about everything. I don't know how to feel or what to do.

I tip my head back against the wall, closing my eyes and pressing my fingers against my temples in an attempt to alleviate the pounding there.

"Do you want me to stay here or do you need a minute to yourself?"

I want him here as much as I want to be alone. It doesn't make sense, so I tell him, "A minute, please."

"Of course." He stands, and I open my eyes to watch him walk toward the door. "Kade mentioned something about a meeting with his sister. I'll go speak with him, and you can join us when you're ready." He gives me one last look, his expression filled with something I can't quite decipher. It's as if he wants to say something more. Instead, he turns and leaves the room, the door clicking shut softly behind him.

I stay on the floor, leaning against the wall and sipping from the glass of water. My head still hasn't stopped spinning, and the more I think about everything that's about to happen, the worse it gets.

I thought being kidnapped and held captive by four vampires would be the most messed up thing to ever happen in my lifetime.

How unbelievably wrong I was.

## 13

## KADE

We spend one more night at the shitty little safe house before hitting the road Friday morning.

No one is in a particularly good mood, and nothing—not even strong coffee and sugary breakfast pastries—is going to help. Between the outcome of the summit and the tension over this meeting with my sister, we're all on edge. That, and I know Calla is worried sick about her human bestie. In hindsight, it might've been better for her to have stayed with us if Atlas is going to waste energy trying to protect her from the attack.

We ride in silence for over an hour. Atlas and Gabriel are up front, with Lex and me in the middle, and Calla is passed out in the very back. It doesn't surprise me. I'd been up several times through the night and could hear her tossing and turning. She wanted to be alone, and none of us pushed it.

I glance at the GPS, my stomach getting queasy as we move closer to our destination. I want to believe I'm not nervous about this meeting, but if it goes anything like the last one...

Nope. Not going there. This time will be different. Everything is on *my* terms. I'm going to get the answers I need to stop my thoughts from spiraling trying to figure out what the hell happened to my sister after she disappeared.

Meredith agreed to meet at a location of my choosing, so Gabriel found a place between the safe house and where we're headed, which apparently is a small town in Connecticut. It's not permanent, but until the hunters are dealt with, we can't return to our home in Washington.

Calla stirs in the back seat, blinking her eyes open and yawning. My dick twitches in response, and I find I have the urge to reach for her. It's a constant desire, really.

Lex glances up from his phone, having heard her wake, and turns to look at her over his shoulder. "Good morning, sleepyhead." He shoots her a wink, to which she responds by covering her face with her arm. Cute.

I reach to the back seat and run my fingers up her arm, circling them around her wrist and prying it away from her face. She grumbles at me, but eventually gives up, opening her eyes.

"Are we there yet?" she mumbles tiredly.

"Almost, angel," Gabriel calls back from the passenger seat. "Just under an hour now."

Hearing that makes my chest tighten, and I grit my teeth. My gaze drops when Calla entwines her fingers through mine.

"You okay?" she whispers, her gaze soft.

I give her hand a squeeze. "You don't need to worry about me."

"But I am worried about you," she says, and her eyes widen slightly, as if she's surprised by her own words.

"Aww, thanks," I tease her, rubbing my thumb over the back of her hand, hanging on tighter when she tries to pull away.

Calla rolls her eyes. "You're so annoying."

"Yeah, but you like me. Admit it."

"I'd rather choke to death on my tongue," she says with a painfully fake smile, tugging on her hand until I let go.

Lex snorts, having turned his attention back to his phone. A quick glance shows me that he's texting back and forth with Marcel about our next safe house to ensure everything is set up for our arrival this afternoon.

Calla's eyes shift between Lex and me. "Can I go back to sleep now?"

"I suppose you could, or I could come back there and we could do something a lot more fun."

She stares at me, trying to keep a straight face, but I don't miss the leap in her pulse. I could back off, but instead, I keep pushing.

"Remember the night of the house party? Sitting in the back of this car with Lex and me on either side of you?"

Her cheeks flush a lovely shade of pink and her refusal to answer only spurs me on.

"No?" My eyes flick between hers, and I unbuckle my seat belt. "Shall we remind you?"

Calla scrambles upright and shoots me a glare. "I remember perfectly." She swallows hard and tucks her legs onto the seat.

Lex pouts without turning back to her. "So no reminder then?"

"You've been staring at your phone this whole time," she says, "I figured you were looking at porn for your spank bank. I don't think you need me."

He pockets his phone and undoes his seat belt, moving into the back seat before I can and before Calla can make a sound of protest. "You severely underestimate your own allure," he says in a low voice, capturing her chin between his fingers.

Calla wets her lips, and the sound of her racing heart pounds through the vehicle. "My *allure*?" She laughs softly. "Is that your weird way of saying I'm better than porn?"

"No competition," he answers without hesitation.

"Gee, thanks," she remarks dryly, knocking his hand away from her face. "Now will you let me go back to sleep?"

"I could," he muses, licking his lips as he holds her gaze, "or I could make you come so hard you'll be energized for the rest of the day."

Her mouth drops open for a moment before she realizes and snaps it shut. You'd think she'd be used to hearing things like that by now—at least from Lex.

"I'm good." She turns her attention out the window next to her, and I shoot Lex a smirk. He flips me off and grabs Calla's ankles, pulling them out from under her and across his lap. She immediately tries to get away, which of course only encourages Lex to trap her against the seat. He makes quick work of unbuckling her seat belt and using it to secure her wrists above her head.

"What the fuck," she snaps. "Cut it out, Lex." She tugs on her wrists and tries to kick him in the stomach. "Let me go."

He winks at her, leaning down until his face is a breath away from hers. "If I thought for a second that's what you actually wanted, I might consider it."

Her eyes narrow sharply, flicking toward me for a moment as her chest heaves from the exertion of trying to break free of her bindings. "Are you enjoying this?"

My lips curl into a grin, and I try to ignore the discomfort of the bulge in my pants. Watching her struggle is getting me hard as fuck. "Not nearly as much as you're about to be."

She stills against the seat and looks back at Lex but says nothing. She has apparently reserved herself to silence.

"What, are we playing the quiet game now?" I ask.

Lex chuckles. "Not for long." He captures Calla's chin, holding her gaze. "Tell me what you want."

Calla stiffens for a brief moment as Lex's glamour slams into her, then visibly relaxes. "I…" The word hisses through her teeth as she tries to fight his glamour.

"Go on," he murmurs, and a quick glance at his crotch shows me how much this is turning him on as well.

Gabriel and Atlas remain silent up front, choosing instead to turn up the music and ignore the three of us.

Her expression is vacant as she stares into his eyes. "I want… you to…" She swallows hard. "Get the fuck off me and quit acting like a damn caveman."

His shocked expression mirrors mine. He pulls back, letting go of her chin, and shakes his head.

My eyes shift between the two. "Did she just—"

"I think so," Lex says without taking his eyes off her.

"I resisted glamour," Calla says, pressing her lips together to hide a smile. She's proud of herself, and I can't really blame her.

"How?" Lex asks, his brows pinching closer.

Calla tugs on her wrists, shooting him a look. "How the hell should I know?" Her legs are still draped over his lap, but she manages to sit up.

"Are you guys listening to this?" I say, looking toward the front of the car.

Atlas's grip on the wheel tightens, and he exchanges a look with Gabriel. "Perhaps the back seat of a moving vehicle isn't the optimal place to explore this," he offers in a tight voice.

"Try it again," Calla says, and my head whips toward her, though she's still looking at Lex.

"Really?" he asks.

She nods. "I want to see if I can do it again."

The corner of his mouth kicks up as he makes the

connection once more. "Tell me the truth," he says in a smooth voice, sliding his hand up her leg. "If I was to slide my hand into your panties right now, how wet would I find you?"

Her jaw clenches and her brows knit in concentration as she actively attempts to fight his glamour. "I'm..." She clears her throat, and her hands curl into fists where they're still bound in the seat belt above her head.

"Tell me," Lex pushes.

A shudder runs through her and she grits her teeth as her cheeks flush, whispering, "I'm soaked."

Lex breaks the connection, his hand wrapped around her thigh. "Good effort." He shoots her a wink.

She rolls her eyes. "Whatever. Can you untie me now?"

"Say please, and I'll consider it." His hand slides higher, and her breath hitches, her gaze dropping to where Lex's fingers inch closer to the apex of her thighs.

"Go to hell," she mutters instead.

He shrugs. "Don't think for a second I won't drag you there with me."

She manages to twist her wrists enough to get one free, but I reach back and catch it before she can take a swing at Lex.

"Ah, ah, ah. Hitting isn't nice," I tell her.

She huffs out a breath, then clamps her mouth shut when Lex cups her through her pants. His thumb presses down, and she bites her lip, staring at the roof of the vehicle.

"Are you going to be a good girl and let me make you come?"

Her eyes snap to his, and she opens her mouth but no words come out. Her pulse is pounding beneath her flushed skin, and I can smell her sweet arousal as clearly as I bet Lex can.

He tilts his head to the side, watching her for a few

seconds before he says, "I'm going to take your silence as a resounding yes." He wastes no time sliding his hand into her pants, and I keep my eyes on her face. Her eyes widen slightly, and she bites her lip so hard I'm waiting for her to bleed.

"Let go," I tell her, my thumb brushing over the pounding pulse at her wrist. "Give yourself over to the pleasure."

She sucks in a sharp breath as Lex pushes his fingers inside her. Twisting her wrist in my grasp, she grabs a hold of me, digging her fingers into my arm. "Fuck," she breathes, her chest rising and falling fast as she opens her legs wider.

"Good girl," Lex says in a voice thick with arousal. "Lift your hips for me."

She complies, and he tugs her leggings and panties halfway to her knees. His thumb presses against her clit as he pumps his fingers in and out of her pussy, filling the car with the smell of her. It makes my gums and my dick throb with the desire to fuck and feed from her.

Lex pulls his fingers out and sticks them in his mouth, sucking them clean before lowering his head between her legs. Calla's grip on my arm tightens when Lex drags his tongue along her slit before swirling it around her clit.

Fucking hell, my dick is rock hard at this point.

Calla lets go of my arm, and I slip into the back seat, guiding her onto her back with my legs spread open on either side of her. It's a bit of a tight squeeze, but Lex hauls her closer to him, making it work. I hiss out a sharp breath when she reaches over her head and palms the front of my pants. She's playing with fire if she thinks she can tease me without following through.

I cover her hand with mine, pressing down harder, and groan. I make quick work of popping the button on my pants and unzipping them before pulling my cock out. Her fingers wrap around it immediately, moving at the perfect rhythm. I desperately want to bury myself between her thighs, but the back seat of Atlas's car isn't exactly conducive to that. Besides, Lex is taking care of that quite well at the moment.

Calla moves her thumb over the head of my cock, using the moisture beading there to glide smoothly up and down my shaft as Lex devours her pussy with his tongue. Her speed picks up as Lex's movements quicken, and pressure builds in my balls as she continues to pump. Her gaze is glued to where Lex is positioned between her legs, and she moans softly, her cheeks bright pink.

"Don't stop," I tell her in a gravelly voice, and her grip tightens a little, making a deep growl tear from my throat and my fangs extend. *Fuck.* I'm going to come any second, and Calla looks to be just as close, her breaths coming in short pants as her heart pounds loudly. "Make her come," I order Lex, fighting the urge to sink my fangs into Calla.

She sucks in a sharp breath, her fingers stilling around my shaft for a few seconds as the sounds of her unbridled moans fill the car. Her fingers start moving again, pumping my cock harder and faster as she comes around Lex's tongue. He stays between her legs, lapping up her release as if it's his last meal on this earth, and I grunt, my muscles tensing as my orgasm whips through me and I come. My release coats Calla's hand and thick ropes trail up the length of her arm.

It takes me a minute to catch my breath and tuck myself back into my pants.

Gabriel offers a handkerchief from the front—because of course Gabriel has a handkerchief—and I clean myself off Calla's skin, while Lex tugs her leggings back up, making sure her dagger is secure, and presses a kiss to her cheek.

"Thanks for the road trip snack," he tells her with a wink.

She groans. "You are so annoying."

"You didn't seem to think so a minute ago." He lowers his voice. "Don't worry. You can get me back later tonight."

She chokes on a laugh. "Don't count on it."

He pouts. "You're so mean to me."

"If you three are done," Atlas calls from the driver's seat, "we'll be arriving in about twenty minutes."

My stomach sinks as panic starts to claw at my chest. I enjoyed the distraction for a little while, but the reality of what we're about to do is settling in again.

"Hey." Calla's soft voice catches my attention, and I meet her gaze. Her eyes flick between mine, and she nods. "Everything is going to be okay."

I force a smile, more grateful for her at this moment than she could possibly understand. I just hope to hell she's right.

❧

The address we sent Meredith to meet us at is an old brewery one of Marcel's contacts owns. It was shut down years ago and is pretty much in the middle of nowhere. We have to drive on a gravel road for the last ten minutes of the trip to reach it, which thrills Atlas to no end; he's always been protective of his car.

My leg bounces as we pull up outside the tall factory building, and Atlas kills the engine.

"You ready, brother?" Lex asks, slapping a hand on my shoulder.

"Not in the slightest," I grumble, turning around in my seat. "Let's get this over with."

The five of us get out of the Escalade, and Atlas steps in front of Calla, blocking her path.

"What is your problem?" she says, crossing her arms as she looks up at him.

"You're staying here."

"The hell I am," she shoots back.

"You'd like to test me?" he asks in a mild tone.

She doesn't back down even when he steps closer, towering over her. "Considering you're being ridiculous, yeah."

Gabriel sighs. "Come on. We're wasting time standing out here."

"Agreed," Atlas says without looking away from Calla. "Get back in the car."

"Fuck off." She moves to step around him, but he grabs her arm and drags her backward. "Atlas!" His name comes out as more of a growl as she attempts to dig her heels into the gravel.

"If we're trying *not* to attract attention, perhaps we should move this inside?" Lex offers, looking rather bored of the whole thing, though I don't miss the way his jaw is clenched or the way his eyes dart around, surveying the area.

Atlas curses under his breath and releases her, turning and prowling toward the building. The rest of us follow him, and Calla shoots daggers at the back of his head. He breaks the deadbolt and unchains the heavy metal door, swinging it open with a loud creak, and we file inside.

The interior of the brewery is dark and cold. Several of the window panes have been smashed out and no doubt the electricity hasn't worked for years. Our steps echo off the concrete floors as we walk around stacks of empty kegs. The scent of yeast and sulfur lingers in the air, so faint I'd guess that Calla can't smell it, but it tickles my nose.

Every tiny sound catches my attention, and my gaze whips around the space. I can't remember a time I've been so on edge. Perhaps when I first turned…

The door creaks open again, and we all turn at the same time.

Daylight streams into the darkness, and Meredith's form is a silhouette in the doorway as she steps inside, letting the door close behind her.

My heart rattles in my chest as she walks closer, and Atlas steps forward. We didn't discuss exactly how we'd handle this meeting, and I didn't tell my sister I wasn't coming alone, though she should have expected as much.

Her silver eyes run the line of us, widening slightly as she takes in the fact she is severely outnumbered. Not to mention, Atlas's reputation precedes him in the vampire community. If I didn't know him, didn't care for him as if he'd been the one to turn me, I'd be scared shitless of the guy.

She steps back, pressing her lips together as the color drains from her face. "Kade," she says in a low voice. "I… I thought we were meeting, um, alone."

"Not a chance," Lex says before I can offer an answer.

Meredith frowns, glancing down and making her black, shoulder-length hair fall forward. She reaches up and tucks it behind her ear. "Right. I guess that's fair."

"Considering you stabbed me last time, I'd say so." I have so much I want to say, to ask, but I can't make the words form. I shake my head. "Why are we meeting, Mer?"

Her eyes move from me to the others and back. "Can we talk somewhere a little more—"

"Nope," Lex cuts in. "Whatever you need to say to your brother, say it now, or you can walk right back through that door."

She blinks quickly. It's almost as if… *Is she going to cry?*

I fight the urge to step forward, to comfort her even after all this time. Even after she ambushed us with the hunters. Because she's still my sister.

Meredith clears her throat, walking closer to our group, stopping once she's a mere few feet away. "Kade," she starts in a low voice. "I… I know you deserve an explanation."

I find myself nodding. "What the hell happened to you, Mer?"

"That is sort of a long story." She takes a deep breath,

tugging the lapels of her denim jacket tighter around her narrow frame. "The night I disappeared, the party I was at was attacked by a group of vampires. Everyone was killed. I should have died that night, but..." Her voice trails off, and she kicks at the concrete floor with a booted foot. "I caught the eye of the vampire leading the group. He was impressed that I was still breathing after having my throat nearly ripped out. So he saved me, fed me his blood, and took me with them. For months, he used me as his personal feeder, until one day... he fed me his blood and then snapped my neck. I was asleep for days, and when I woke, my throat was on fire. I had this unquenchable thirst and I... I was so scared. I quickly realized that I'd been turned into the very monster that had stolen my life."

I'm clenching my jaw so hard, my gums are throbbing and tension is building in my temples. My hands curl into fists, and I shove them into my jeans.

"It took me almost a decade to get a handle on my blood-lust." Her gaze drops to the floor, and she sighs. "I killed a lot of people figuring it out."

"What about the vampire who turned you?" Gabriel asks.

Meredith shrugs. "What about him? Once I woke and found out what he did to me, I fled. I didn't want to be part of the group of monsters that found entertainment in slaughtering random college students just trying to have a good time on a Friday night."

"Fine," Lex chimes in. "You became a vampire, struggled to adjust, and then joined forces with the very people who wish to eradicate our kind?"

Her eyes hold mine despite Lex's words. "I allied with the hunters to protect myself."

I frown at her. "Protecting yourself from the hunters?" If Selene had done it, maybe we need to consider that other vampires have as well.

She hesitates, then shakes her head. "From my sire. Turns out he didn't take too kindly to me running from him. He tried to track me down a few times, but I'd made friends among the hunters. They took care of him for me."

Anger pulls at me, and a muscle ticks in my jaw. "Did you know when I became a vampire?"

Meredith presses her lips together before nodding. "Of course. I kept tabs on my family. I witnessed the devastation our parents experienced when I went missing, when they never found me." She blinks quickly, her eyes glassy. "I was there the day the three of you buried my empty casket."

"We looked for you," I say, my voice uneven. "Months went by, and the police were no help whatsoever. I didn't want to give up, but they… Our parents needed closure, Mer. *I* needed closure. We were looking for someone we were never going to find." Recalling that time makes my head spin and my stomach churn, especially now knowing what really happened to my sister.

She nods. "But you didn't know that back then. I was still out there."

"So why didn't you return home?" Atlas speaks up.

Her eyes snap to him. "I couldn't. It wasn't safe. Even once I'd gotten a grip on my hunger and the urge to tear into the throats of everyone I passed on the street, my sire was still out there." Meredith turns her gaze back to me. "If I went home to my family, I would be putting them all at risk. He'd come after me and hunt you all just to get back at me for leaving him. And after the hunters killed him, I thought about going home to be with my family, but I… I couldn't do it."

Gabriel exhales softly, and I don't have to turn my gaze toward him to know there's a look of sympathy on his face.

"So you just let us believe you were dead?" I snap before I can stop myself.

Her gaze hardens. "After everyone gave up on finding me, yes I did, brother. And I was angry, so fucking livid. I could forgive Mom and Dad. They were weak and broken before I disappeared. But you…" Her chin quivers. "You just let them give up on me. *You* gave up on me."

I swallow the lump of emotion in my throat and force out, "Is that why you stabbed me?"

She exhales a humorless laugh. "Perhaps. That blond vampire, Selene, told the hunters about you lot. I knew I had to see you before they wiped you out, so I volunteered to lead the ambush. I was meant to kill you to distract the others so that when the hunters attacked, they'd be successful in killing you all."

A growl rumbles through Lex's chest, and he starts to move forward until Atlas grabs him, pulling him back without a word.

Meredith clasps her hands together, sniffling. "I couldn't do it. I knew the moment I saw you, I wouldn't be able to go through with it."

"But you still stabbed me."

She nods. "I was still angry."

A laugh escapes my lips. "And now?"

"I've had time to process everything with a clearer head and I…" She looks away, lowering her voice. "I want to know my little brother."

My chest fills with pressure and my throat feels as if it's closing in. My heartbeat kicks up and my eyes search hers, looking for any hint of dishonesty. There's nothing in her gaze but fear and longing. I believe she's telling the truth, and I want to know her too.

"What about the hunters?" Lex demands. "You think you can just walk away from them?"

She spares him a glance. "I've gotten pretty good at running." She looks back at me and steps closer. "What do you think? Can we forgive one another and be part of each other's lives? Eternity is a long time to live without family."

"He *has* a family," Calla snaps, speaking up for the first time.

Meredith's eyes go to her, and she offers a faint smile. "You're human."

Calla crosses her arms over her chest, standing taller. "Do you have a point or do you just like stating the obvious?"

Lex snorts and Gabriel rests a hand on Calla's shoulder.

Meredith blinks in surprise. "She's a bit mouthy, isn't she?"

"A bit," Lex echoes with a laugh, and Calla shoots him a glare.

Meredith focuses on me again. "What do you say, baby bro? Will you give us a chance to get to know each other again?"

I blow out a breath, nerves swirling in my stomach like a wicked hurricane. I haven't felt so entirely out of my element in decades. "Yeah," I finally say after several beats of heavy silence. "I'd like that."

Between one moment and then next, Meredith closes the remaining distance between us and wraps her arms around me. I stiffen in response, and it takes a few long moments before I relax enough to hug her back. There's a new kind of pressure in my chest, and I think it might be hope.

Then the brewery doors fly open, breaking off their hinges, and hunters flood the room.

Betrayal whips through me as everything moves in slow motion. Lex grabs Calla, shoving her toward Gabriel before storming forward with Atlas, fangs bared. Gabriel catches Calla easily and moves her behind him, putting himself between her and the mob of angry humans.

The sound of daggers being unsheathed rings in my ears as I look toward my sister. My stomach plummets when I catch the look of shock and horror on her face. She wasn't expecting us to be ambushed, which means... she didn't betray me this time.

No time to think about that now. I reach for her, wrapping my fingers around her wrist and pulling her toward me within seconds of her ending up with a dagger in her chest.

Three hunters close in on us, and Meredith growls at the curvy blond one. "What are you doing?" she hisses despite it being painfully obvious. They're here to wipe us out and they used my sister to track us down.

Blondie doesn't answer her. Instead, she swipes the air in front of her with her dagger, making us move backward.

Several more hunters spill into the room, bringing the total to at least a dozen. My eyes shift between them, then move to where Atlas is tearing into the throat of a middle-aged hunter. His blood sprays across the concrete floor, and Atlas tosses his lifeless body aside, moving onto the next target.

"Kade." Meredith's voice shakes, and I snap my attention back to the small group of hunters attempting to back us into a corner. *I think the fuck not.*

"Get behind me," I bark at her, my fangs slicing through my gums.

"No way," she snaps back, baring her own fangs at me.

"Fine," I say through my teeth, "then get ready to fight."

Before I can move, she snarls and launches herself forward, grabbing the blond hunter by her hair, yanking her head back and sinking her fangs into the woman's throat. She cries out in pain, and the other two hunters descend. Not quick enough. I move in a blur, grabbing both of them by their throats, then slam their heads together, effectively knocking them out cold.

Meredith drops the hunter to the floor near the others,

and she moans, her eyelids fluttering as she struggles to stay conscious.

We immediately jump into the thick of the fight, where Lex is facing off with a hunter whose arms have to be even thicker than mine, which is saying something. He's managed to get a few good hits in; Lex has blood leaking from a gash over his eye and rolling down his chin.

"Kade, behind you!" Calla's voice slices through the sounds of fighting, high-pitched and filled with panic. *What the fuck is she still doing here?*

I whirl around just in time to block the dagger that was headed for my heart. Meredith snarls and kicks the hunter's legs out from under him. She doesn't hesitate—between one second and the next, she snaps his neck, dropping his body carelessly and stepping over it.

I find myself shaking my head, wanting to close my eyes and erase the picture of my sister slaughtering these people despite their intentions for us. Seeing my sister as the same monster that looks back at me in the mirror has my blood running cold and my heart cracking in my chest. I don't want this life for her. But it's too late.

Another swarm of hunters marches inside, and Atlas and Lex tear their way through them, only experiencing minor injuries. Nothing a little blood won't heal in a matter of minutes.

Gabriel hangs back, guarding Calla, while Meredith and I charge forward to back up the others. The smell of human blood is overwhelming. We're all covered in it. The monster that lives inside me revels in this chaos. My lips twist into a dark grin as I grab another hunter, a pretty brunette one. Her eyes widen, but she doesn't have a chance to beg for mercy before I rip through her windpipe and shove her toward another oncoming hunter. He's younger, probably seventeen or eighteen, and his eyes are as wide as saucers when he catches the still body of his fallen comrade.

Two hunters move around him, charging toward me. I slide out of the way, and when I turn to take them on, I freeze. They managed to grab hold of Meredith. My world narrows on them, on the dagger they have poised over her heart.

"Let her go, and I'll end your pathetic life quickly," I say slowly in a low voice, a muscle ticking in my jaw.

The hunter shrugs as if he doesn't care either way and drops his arm with the dagger as the guy on her other side rolls his eyes.

Meredith frowns briefly and takes a step forward. Her entire body goes rigid, and panic floods through me. It's swiftly replaced by white-hot pain and fury when a third hunter attacks from behind, shoving his dagger through her back until it protrudes from her chest. He yanks it out, replacing it with his hand. Meredith shrieks in agony… until the sound is cut off as the hunter pulls back with her blood-covered heart in his hand.

The sounds of battle behind me fade as I watch my sister fall to her knees, her face turning gray as the life leaves her eyes. And then her heart hits the floor with a sickening *thump.*

I see red. I give myself over to the monster wholly, letting it control me as I black out with rage and tear through the rest of the hunters.

At some point, Atlas pulls me back, and I stumble, unable to fight any more. It takes me a few seconds to refocus, and I frown at the figure stepping through the open doorway.

Calla sucks in a sharp breath, her hand wrapped around Gabriel's arm and her pulse pounding like a jackhammer.

"Well, this is quite disappointing," Scott Ellis says, rubbing a hand along his neatly trimmed beard. He's dressed in the same all-black uniform as the rest of the hunters, but he makes no move to join in on the fight.

At least half a dozen more hunters filter in behind him, poised with daggers and ready to fight.

Fucking hell, it never ends.

Atlas steps forward, intentionally blocking Calla from view, and wipes the blood from his mouth. "My sentiments exactly."

Scott frowns, his eyes moving past Atlas and filling with confusion. "Calla?" Anger flares to life in his gaze as he looks at each of us. "What are you doing with her?" he growls.

"Nothing she doesn't enjoy," Lex says with a smirk.

"Lex," Atlas snaps. The *this isn't the time* is unspoken, but it's certainly clear in his tone.

Scott ignores them both, focusing on Calla. "It's going to be okay. I'll get you out of here and away from these monsters."

The hunters flanking him charge forward, and I prepare myself to rip these motherfuckers to shreds. But I don't get the chance. Gabriel appears in front of the rest of us and goes absolutely ballistic.

I've known Gabriel for over a century, and never in that time have I seen him like this. He slaughters the hunters in a matter of seconds. Blood and organs paint the dirty floor, and the hunters' fearless leader runs out the door while the rest of us are enamored by Gabriel's equally graceful and lethal attack.

"Fuck," Lex snaps. "More are coming. We have to get the hell out of here."

Leave. We need to leave.

This place is filled with the bodies of almost two dozen hunters.

And my sister.

I can't tear my eyes away from her. The image is burned into my mind for the rest of my immortal life.

Lex's voice sounds far away when he says, "We need to leave *now*. Before the rest of the bastards show up."

"I'll deal with Scott and grab the car. Meet me around the back of the building," Atlas says in a voice that is dangerously calm, then quickly disappears through the doorway outside.

Calla appears in front of me and reaches for my face. "Kade," her voice is soft, so soft I want to close my eyes and wrap myself in it. To forget every other fucking thing and just exist with her in a world where I didn't just watch my sister get her heart ripped out.

"Let's go, brother," Gabriel says.

Between him, Lex, and Calla, they manage to drag me away from the piles of bodies.

Everything from that moment until we're speeding down the interstate is a blur. I stare out the window from the back seat, barely feeling Calla's fingers slide through mine. She squeezes, and I'm not sure if she's trying to get my attention, but I can't bring myself to look at her.

Losing my sister the first time just about ruined me. I can't fathom how I'll survive it a second time.

## 14

## CALLA

My heart hurts for Kade. For everything he's been through and the sister he lost after coming so close to getting her back. She was ripped away, and there wasn't a thing he could do to stop it.

As I stare at him, the desire to take away his pain—to bring it on myself even—is jarring. It's something I wasn't expecting and am not sure what to do with. It buries itself deep in my chest, digging its claws in until I force myself to look away from Kade.

By the time we reach Monroe, Connecticut, we've driven through the darkest part of the night.

Atlas, as usual, is behind the wheel. Kade is next to him in the passenger seat, staring blankly out the windshield as the headlights illuminate the road in front of us. There are no other vehicles around us, making the atmosphere eerie, especially paired with the layer of misty fog we're traveling through.

Lex is passed out across the seat behind Gabriel and me, snoring softly. Under different circumstances, it would be cute. But here we are running for our lives—again.

And now Brighton's dad knows I'm involved with the vampires, which really isn't something we need. I can't be sure what he'll do. Will he bring it up to Brighton with the expectation that I told her about the vampires? Should I text her? If Scott wasn't monitoring her phone before, I'd bet good money he is now.

I try to close my eyes and get some rest, but it's useless. My stomach is so twisted in knots, and despite the fact I didn't participate in the fight at the brewery, I still somehow ended up covered in blood. We all are, and it's all I can smell. Atlas's poor car is going to need to be deep cleaned at this point.

The sun is just starting to rise when we pass the town sign welcoming us to Monroe.

"It's a quiet place to lay low for a while," Gabriel says in a soft voice.

When I turn toward him, he's already looking at me. "Right. How many vampires are in this town?"

"Four," Atlas says from up front, turning down a residential street where the streetlights are flickering, stuck in that period between night and day.

Four?

*Oh.*

These guys are the only vampires in town.

"Is that safe?" I watch out my window as we pass by gorgeous houses, both uniform yet slightly unique, with perfectly manicured lawns on both sides of the street. "I mean, a small town filled with only humans… Won't that attract attention we're not looking for?"

"It's okay," Gabriel assures me. "Marcel set us up with a rental property in a neighborhood with mostly young professionals. We shouldn't stick out, and—"

"And hopefully, we won't be here long enough for it to be a problem."

My eyes shift from Gabriel to the back of Atlas's head. "Okay." I don't have much of a choice but to trust them. "What about blood? Does Marcel have a contact at the local blood bank or something?"

Gabriel offers me a faint smile.

"Of course he does," I say under my breath.

Atlas slows as we reach the end of the street, which I'm realizing now is a cul-de-sac, and pulls into a circular driveway, stopping the car outside a stunning colonial home.

Gabriel reaches behind us and shakes Lex awake as the others get out of the front. I climb out of the back with the intention of grabbing Kade's hand, but he's already halfway up the porch steps when my feet hit the paved driveway. I frown as he reaches under a mat on the porch and pulls out a key, opening the front door and disappearing inside.

"He needs some time."

I jump at the sound of Atlas's voice at my ear, then turn my head to look at him. "I want to help. He doesn't deserve to be in this pain."

Atlas's tired eyes flick between mine and he nods in understanding. He reaches for me, placing his hand at the middle of my back, and guides me toward the house.

The floors and doors are dark wood and the walls are a pristine white. It feels classic and elegant and definitely not a place five people in bloodstained clothing should be occupying.

"We need to wash our clothes," I announce around a yawn and tug my shirt off over my head.

"I see a very kinky game of strip poker in our future," Lex says with a grin as his eyes drop to my chest.

I cover myself up and roll my eyes. "It's like seven in the morning. Can you chill?"

The guys strip to their boxers, leaving their shoes on the porch. I do the same and step out of my pants, collecting everything and wandering through the house until I find the laundry room at the back of it. Once our clothes are in the washing machine, I wander back toward the front and find the others in what appears to be a formal living room with stiff furniture and a massive white brick fireplace but no TV.

"Home sweet home," I mutter, dropping onto the floral patterned couch next to Gabriel. It feels all kinds of wrong to be sitting around nearly naked with three sexy as hell men in an unfamiliar house.

"Not for long," Lex says in a low voice. "Once the hunters are wiped out, we can return to our actual home." I find myself missing the mansion. At first, I hated the place. It was my gilded cage. But at some point—and I'm not sure when exactly—it became more than that. Nowhere has truly felt like *home* to me—certainly not the city I grew up in—but it could have. Maybe it still could.

"Let's not get ahead of ourselves," Gabriel says.

I open my mouth to question what's going to happen next when my phone chimes from where I left it in the laundry room. With a sigh, I get up and retrieve it. My pulse jumps when I see Brighton's name on the screen. I snatch up my phone and read her message, holding my breath the whole time.

*Do you have any idea why my dad is asking a million questions about you and how we met, when we met, where we met? He's being super freaking weird, Cal.*

I lean against the washing machine, chewing my bottom lip as I try to come up with a response that isn't going to make her freak out more.

*What did you tell him?* I type back.

*Not much. The truth, which he already knew. That we met at school in freshman year.*

Before I can type out a reply, another message comes through.

*Something is going on, I can feel it. He's sending me and my mom on a vacation out of nowhere and he's not coming with us. It doesn't make sense. He doesn't know that I know about the vampires...*

I blow out a heavy breath and craft a response that details what went down at the brewery and what the old vampires have planned for the hunters. I don't disclose our location, but I tell her we're hiding out until the attack the vampires have planned. I also add that she can't tell her dad any of this, though it seems as if he already knows about the looming attack.

*My head is going to explode.*

I exhale a short, humorless laugh at her message. As much as I hate that Brighton is now somewhat involved in this crazy mess, I'm glad to be able to talk to my best friend about it. But it also means I have to live with the fear that she's going to end up hurt because of it—because of me.

*Same here. But seriously, you and your mom should go. Things are going to get ugly fast, and you shouldn't be around for it.*

If Scott somehow got tipped off that the vampires are planning an attack in a couple of days, we could have a problem. Well, the vampires could. This really isn't my fight, though I'm forced to watch the outcome either way.

*We're going, don't worry. Are you sure you're safe?*

No. I'll probably never be *safe* as long as I live in a world with vampires.

*Yes*, I write back.

*Good*, she replies. A moment later, another message comes through. *I'm going to lose my dad, aren't I?"*

Her words feel like a punch to my gut, and I blink back the tears that prick my eyes. How am I supposed to answer that? She already knows the answer, but I think she needs someone else to tell her. To confirm her fears.

*I don't know for sure, but there's a very good chance, yes.*

Brighton's reply doesn't come until five minutes later. My chest feels tight until the phone buzzes in my hand, and then my stomach sinks.

*I appreciate your honesty. Something's going down here. I'll text you later.*

My fingers hover over the screen as if I'm going to type a response, but nothing comes. I guess there's not much else to say at this point.

I walk out of the laundry room, stopping outside of the main floor bathroom, and find a linen closet. I reach up on my tiptoes, grabbing a black fleece blanket and wrapping it around myself before returning to the living room where Atlas is starting a fire in the fireplace.

"Brighton's father knows something," I say as I walk back to the couch. Within seconds, I have three sets of silver eyes staring at me expectantly. "He's sending Brighton and her mom away."

A muscle feathers along Atlas's jaw, and he grabs his phone off the mantle, lifting it to his ear as he walks out of the room.

I frown, turning toward Gabriel. "Do you think Scott knows about the plan for attack?"

He reaches toward me, resting his hand on my knee over the blanket. "It could mean that or any number of other things. Seeing you shocked him and could very well be why he's sending them away. If he thinks you're tied to us, he could be acting proactively to protect his family."

I glance from where his hand rests on my knee to his face. "From me?" I ask, my brows pinching together.

"I don't know, angel, but we're going to figure it out."

"Isn't your bestie not being around when the vamps attack her daddy a good thing?" Lex asks, lounging sideways in the wingback chair next to the fireplace. He stares at the flames, drumming his fingers on his bare thighs.

"That's not the point," I tell him. I may not agree with what Scott is doing, but Brighton doesn't deserve to lose her dad.

He only shrugs in response, and I'm reminded once again that the vampires I'm bound to couldn't care less about Brighton. They're only concerned about the threat posed by her family and the rest of the hunters. I've never felt so stuck in the middle before, concerned both for my best friend and the vampires I've come to care for over the last month and a half of being with them.

I can't just sit in this room that reminds me of a fucking museum and stare at the wall, so I get off the couch, deciding to explore this place we'll be staying in until we can go back to Washington.

The entire place is elegant but old fashioned. With crown molding and oil paintings on the walls. It's kind of creepy, like a dollhouse... until I wander downstairs to the basement. I'm expecting concrete floors and total darkness, so imagine my surprise when I find a theater room with plush black recliners and a giant projector screen built into the wall.

Okay, this totally makes up for the lack of TV in the living room upstairs.

I step into the room and find the remote, turning on the screen and finding it hooked up to some sort of system that has every streaming service imaginable. If I had to guess, we probably have Marcel to thank for this. I haven't met the guy yet, but he seems to work magic to help the guys—and me too, I suppose.

I flip through the different streaming services and find a serial killer documentary that I haven't seen yet. I've been a little too preoccupied to keep up with new true crime releases. Turning it on, I flop into the middle recliner in the front row, snuggling in with my blanket and using the remote to turn the lights down.

The show is about a half hour in when Lex's voice startles me.

"What in the fucking hell? Have I entered an alternate reality?"

I chuckle, pausing the documentary and turning to find him standing in the doorway, stunned as I was upon finding this room. "Right?"

His eyes flick to the screen, and he arches a brow. "What are you watching?"

Pressing my lips together, I hesitate before saying, "Uh, it's a true crime documentary."

Amusement fills his features, and he walks into the room, dropping into the seat next to mine. "I knew you were dark like me," he says, shooting me a wink.

I roll my eyes. "You can only stay if you're not going to talk through the whole thing."

Lex presses his hand to his chest, his expression now serious. "You have my word."

"Yeah, okay," I remark dryly, turning my attention back to the screen.

"You going to share that blanket? My clothes are still in the dryer."

"Do you want to share my chair too?" Sarcasm drips from my tone, and Lex laughs. Without warning, he stands and scoops me up before sitting back in my spot—with me in his lap.

"You're right. This is definitely much better." He's grinning down at me, his breath soft against my forehead.

Heat fills my face as his lower half presses into me, and I shake my head, hoping my hair will hide the blush in my cheeks. "I didn't... Never mind." I turn the show back on and slowly relax in Lex's arms.

Halfway through the show, my eyelids start to feel heavy. They flutter as I yawn, and Lex's arms tighten around me.

His lips brush the shell of my ear as he says, "We're watching a show where they're describing how this guy brutally slaughtered a bunch of people, and you're all cozy and trying not to fall asleep."

"Hey," I grumble, "don't judge. Serial killer documentaries relax me."

"Of course they do," he says, and I can hear the grin in his voice without looking at his face.

"Whatever. You're sporting a hard-on, so I'm not sure how you get off mocking me."

"I'd be happy to show you how I get off," he says in a low voice, nipping my earlobe.

My pulse leaps, and I immediately regret my choice of words. "Lex..."

"Hmm?" He nuzzles my neck, dragging his mouth across my skin, licking and kissing as my heart kicks up. The only thing between us is the blanket I'm wrapped in and some flimsy undergarments.

"What are you doing?" I ask, my voice a little breathy.

He slides his hands under the blanket, and the cool air makes me shiver before his fingers touch my bare skin, brushing up and down my sides. "Exactly what you want me to," he answers, gliding one hand up to slide under my bra and cup my breast while the other moves slowly, heading for the heat gathering between my thighs.

I pull in a shallow breath, tilting my head back against Lex's shoulder and closing my eyes. The voices from the documentary fade into the background as I lose myself in Lex's touch, letting everything else fall away. His skilled fingers tweak my nipples and massage my breasts, alternating from one side to the other while his other hand hovers at the thin lace of my panties.

My clit throbs with need, and I quickly grow so impatient

that I grab his hand and guide it into my panties, moaning softly when his fingers brush my folds.

"You know exactly what you want, don't you?"

I arch my back, pushing my breast into his hand. "Right now, I want you to stop talking."

He chuckles, pinching my nipple so hard a spike of pain flashes through the pleasure filling me. "Then I'm going to need *you* to talk. Tell me exactly what you want, and if you're a good girl for me, maybe I'll let you come."

Boldness grips me—I have no idea from where—and I say, "I want you to do whatever you want to me. To take complete control even when I try to fight you. *Show* me what I want." I'm tired of having to say what I want. For once, I want to be told. Because fuck, I need to not have to think for a while.

Lust flares in his liquid silver gaze as he settles me in between his legs. There's something else there too. Something that steals the breath from my lungs. *Hunger.*

"You want me to fuck you into submission?" he taunts in a low voice, running his middle finger along my slit. "I am more than happy to oblige."

Everything in me tightens and my entire body flushes with heat. I'm suddenly too warm in the blanket, and my heart is pounding in my chest.

"You like the sound of that, don't you?" He dips his finger inside easily, gliding through the moisture already gathered there.

"Y-yes," I whisper.

His lips find my neck again, grazing faintly over my pulse. "Open for me."

I spread my legs, making the blanket fall open. The cool air tickles my bare skin, and I suck in a breath when Lex pushes deeper into my pussy, adding another finger and working my clit with his thumb. My hips grind against his fingers, trying to get him even deeper, but he snakes an arm around my waist, holding me still. I struggle against him, trying to feed the friction between my legs, but he stills his fingers inside me.

"Settle down," he murmurs, his lips moving up to brush my ear.

I shiver but keep my mouth shut.

Lex resumes pumping in and out of me, keeping his arm trapped around my waist, and I bite the inside of my cheek when his erection presses into my back. He increases the speed of his thrusts, curling his fingers and hitting my most sensitive spot. I grip the arms of the recliner on either side of us, my breathing coming in short pants as he works me to the brink of orgasm. Pressure builds low in my stomach, my muscles tightening and my pussy clenching around his fingers as he pushes me to climax.

"That's it," Lex says in my ear, "give it to me."

I cry out, gripping his thighs as pleasure spikes through me so intense I can't feel my legs. I come hard on his fingers, and he continues pulsing them inside me, rubbing my pussy walls as I ride the delicious aftershocks of my orgasm.

I squirm in his grasp when he pulls his fingers out, and my stomach clenches when he lifts them to his lips and licks them clean.

"You really are my favorite flavor." He drops his hands to my hips and lifts me easily, turning me in his lap so I'm facing him, straddling his legs. "Now," he says, lifting his hips enough to tug his boxers down, freeing his thick cock, "you're going to take all of me inside you and you're not going to come until I allow it. Understand?"

I swallow hard, my throat suddenly dry. "I... Okay."

Lex offers a dark smirk that makes me lower my gaze away from his. "Good answer." His voice is filled with power and control, making it almost embarrassingly easy to follow his every command. It's exactly what I needed, and it's making me so fucking hot, I couldn't deny it if I wanted to.

Licking my lips I lift myself up as Lex positions the head of his cock at my entrance. I grip his shoulders to keep steady and slowly start to lower myself onto his shaft, letting out a soft moan the deeper he fills me. My pussy stretches to accommodate his size, and I squeeze my eyes shut, focusing on my breathing as I sink the rest of the way onto him.

"Mmm, fuck, you feel so good wrapped around my cock. I can feel you throbbing and tightening around me. You're doing so good."

My previous release makes moving up and down his shaft easier, and I blush at the feel of it leaking down my thighs.

"Again," he orders, capturing my chin with his fingers and bringing my mouth to his. His lips devour mine as I lift up and sink back onto him once more, shivering at how deep he reaches at this angle.

We find a steady rhythm as our lips battle for control, and he pushes his tongue past my lips, flicking it across the roof of my mouth. When his grip on my hips tightens and he starts pushing me down harder on his cock, my pulse jackhammers, and I moan into his mouth. My head spins faster with each thrust, and Lex doesn't ease up at any point. Instead, he lifts his hips, thrusting up into me as I bare down on him. The pressure and friction quickly builds to a near unbearable level, and his lips pull away from my mouth, trailing along my jaw before his fangs graze my neck, teasing the pulse there.

"Lex," I breathe, my heart fighting to break free of my rib cage.

"Stay right there," he says in a thick voice, slamming his hips upward, pushing himself so deep it knocks the air out of me with a shallow gasp. "Don't come yet. I want you on the edge until I'm ready to come inside you."

His words ignite an indescribable pleasure that shoots straight to my core. I throw my head back, moaning without reservation as I continue riding his cock, my breasts bouncing in front of his face.

"I'm so close," I pant, whimpering when Lex reaches between us and strums my clit.

Lex groans. "Not yet." He pulls me against his chest and continues thrusting his hips. His lips find my neck and he sinks his fangs in, drinking deeply as I cry out in a mixture of pleasure and pain. The latter lasts mere seconds before my whole body is flooded with the most euphoric sensation, I can't hold back any longer. He pulls back a moment later, kissing me hard, his lips tasting of copper.

"I'm… *fuck*, I'm going to—"

"Come for me." Lex thrusts hard, his cock throbbing inside me. "*Now*."

I cry out my release as my pussy clenches around him, and he grunts loudly, announcing his own climax as he shoots his release into me.

"Holy shit," I breathe, catching my breath with Lex's cock still buried between my thighs. I feel wickedly energized but lethargic at the same time.

Lex smirks at me. "You are amazing. The feel of you wrapped around my cock… I could fuck you for hours."

I shiver at the thought. "Hmm, well as nice as that sounds, this human could use a bit of recovery time. Maybe a nap and some food."

He leans in and kisses my cheek, chuckling softly. "I suppose we can arrange that." He lifts me off his cock and stands, carrying me toward the staircase as the documentary continues in the background.

## ❧ 15 ☙

# KADE

I open my eyes to darkness outside the window next to the bed I fell into hours ago. Hunger rips through me like fire in my veins, making me shoot upright and swing my legs over the side of the bed. It takes longer than it should for me to remember where we are. To remember what happened that led us here.

I suddenly wish I was still unconscious.

Getting up, I find my clothes clean and folded at the end of the bed. I put them on and make my way back to the main floor of the house. The sound of steady breathing from the bedrooms upstairs tells me everyone else is asleep, and the clock on the stainless steel stove in the kitchen makes me realize why. It's nearly three in the morning.

With a sigh, I open the fridge, grateful to find that Marcel's blood bank contact came through and stocked us up. I snatch a bag of B-positive and let the door close, then search the cupboards for a glass, which I proceed to fill halfway with blood and the rest of the way with whiskey from a bottle I can say with confidence Gabriel left on the counter.

I sit at the head of the old oak table in the attached dining room overlooking the yard. Thick trees line the area, making it feel more private despite being in a residential neighborhood.

Downing half of my drink, my hand shakes as I return the glass to the table. My chest is filled with pressure I haven't experienced in a very long time, and I struggle to ignore the burn of tears in my eyes. I stare hard out the window, into the darkness, begging it to consume me.

I wince when my fangs slice through my gums and cut into my bottom lip. I wipe the blood away and take another drink.

The hunters will pay for what they did. I don't care what Meredith promised them, or even that she stabbed me. I was given the chance to have a life with my sister—my family— and they took it from me.

I'm so lost in anger, I don't hear anyone approach.

"You're going to break that glass if you hold it any tighter," Calla says in a soft, sleep-filled voice.

Even in the dark, wrapped in a bedsheet, she looks angelic. Perhaps I understand a little more why Gabriel is constantly calling her *angel*.

She steps closer, the moonlight from the window next to me illuminating her features, and I quickly turn away, not wanting her to see my face—my fangs or the tears in my eyes. I take another drink, setting the glass down in a steadier motion this time.

"Hey." Calla walks around the table and stops in front of me. "Don't hide from me." She kneels, placing her hands on my knees. "You said that to me once, remember?"

As if I would forget any moment that involved her, especially considering it didn't involve clothing.

I swallow past the thick, suffocating feeling in my throat and finally meet her gaze. "Of course," I murmur.

Her lips curl into a faint smile. "Good." She lowers her gaze a moment, her lashes fanning her cheeks. "Kade, I don't know what to say or do. I… I want to help you."

I slip a finger under her chin, tilting her head up so I can look at her face again. "I appreciate that."

Her eyes search my face. "I can't imagine the pain you're going through. I've never had a sibling, so I don't understand that kind of bond. Do you want to talk about it?"

"No." My voice is hoarse. What I *want* is to rip into the throats of every hunter on this earth. An unrealistic goal, maybe, but the rage simmering inside me is only growing more intense. The bloodlust searing my veins is like nothing I've experienced before, not even when I first turned. I want them all dead. I want to bathe in their blood and listen to the sweet sound of their terrified screams as I end their lives. Every single fucking one of them.

"Okay," she says, her voice filled with understanding. She stands and grabs the chair closest to her, sitting with her knees brushing mine. "What can I do?"

I try to smile, to show her how much it means that she wants to bring me comfort, even after everything *she's* been through. "Distract me. Let's talk about something else." I don't enjoy daydreaming about mass murder when Calla is looking at me with soft eyes. I want to shield her from the monster inside me.

"Um, okay." She chews her bottom lip before flicking her gaze up to meet mine. "Tell me about how you became a vampire."

I stare at her, my eyes widening. "Are you sure you want to know?"

She tucks her legs onto the chair, sitting cross-legged, and nods. "I know Gabriel was turned by Selene and Lex was turned by Atlas, but I don't know your story and I'd like to."

I've never told anyone the story of how I turned, but I

find myself wanting to share with Calla. We know everything about her life; the least I can do is tell her about mine. How I came to be what I am now.

She must take my silence as reluctance to share, because she reaches for my hands and says, "You don't have to tell me, Kade."

I lace my fingers through hers and give her hands a gentle squeeze. "I want to. I'm afraid it's not some dramatic or heartbreaking story, though. You might be disappointed."

Calla arches a brow at me. "Why do you say that?"

"Because," I say, "I became a vampire by accident."

Her eyes widen, and she presses her lips together to try and hide a laugh. "I don't understand." She shakes her head. "How does one *accidentally* become a vampire?"

"As a human, I had a group of friends that happened to be vampires. I suppose the company I kept was a bit of a hazard in itself."

She gives me a knowing look. "Right."

I acknowledge the look with a nod and add, "They didn't make a habit of it or anything, but on occasion they'd feed on me. It was fun. Most of the time we were drunk—they enjoyed the blood and I enjoyed the bite." I meet her gaze. "I know you understand that part." I can see the tinge of pink in her cheeks even in the dim light of the dining room.

"So, what?" she says, freeing her hands from mine and leaning against the back of the chair. "One of them turned you?"

"Not exactly." I pull in a deep breath, let it out, then tap into my memory of my last night as a human.

⊗

*The club is rowdier than normal tonight. The line wound around the block, though our group walked right through the front door as* soon as we arrived. Perks of my friends being able to glamour the doorman.

Will and James head for the bar immediately, while I stick with Sophia and Marianne. They're laughing with their arms draped over each other, murmuring too low for me to hear over the music.

Sweat and booze cling to the air, together with the heavy scent of tobacco. It makes my head swim as the girls start dancing around me, laughing and chatting about the new jewelry they picked up at the market earlier. The guys return a few minutes later, and Will sticks a drink in my hand.

We drink and dance for hours, lost in the lights and the music... until Sophia catches the eye of a man at the bar. He saunters over, trying to get her to dance with him. She's polite at the beginning, smiling and waving him away, but the longer he persists, the more agitated she becomes. She can handle herself, there's no doubt in my mind, but the scene playing out before me makes me think of my sister, of whatever happened the night she disappeared.

My eyes dart around, looking for the others, but I don't see them anywhere. I'm stepping in between Sophia and the drunk man before I can stop myself. I shove him back hard, putting distance between him and Sophia, which only pisses him off. His face is red with anger and maybe some embarrassment as we seem to have attracted a bit of a crowd.

"Back off," I snarl at the burly man.

He barks out a laugh and comes at me, his muddy brown eyes bloodshot. "Take your own advice before I snap you in half, mate." His eyes shift back to Sophia. "No need to worry, gorgeous. I'll take you back to mine and show you a real good time."

His words set off a rage in my chest I've never felt before, and I swing my fist toward his face. My punch snaps his head back as pain flares through my knuckles, and I curse under my breath.

"Kade!" Sophia's voice slices through the music and the crowd.

When the man's group of friends rushes over, flanking him, I have the sense to know I might've made a mistake.

*Everything happens so fast. The group of guys closes in on me, slamming their fists into my face, chest, and gut, and at some point, I end up on the grimy tile floor, being kicked in the stomach.*

*I spit blood out, groaning, which is easily drowned out by the yelling, and before long, someone is hauling me to my feet. My one eye is almost swollen shut already, but I faintly recognize the silver-eyed man practically carrying me through the room, the sounds fading in and out around me.*

*James kicks the door to the men's room open and shouts at the few guys in there to get out. Once we're alone, he locks the door and sets me on the bench next to it, capturing my chin and tilting my head back to look into my eyes.*

*"You got yourself into quite the battle."*

*I groan in response, letting my head fall back against the wall. I feel like a complete idiot. Sophia could have easily dealt with that disgusting man all on her own, but I decided she shouldn't have to.*

*James pats my cheek, and I wince at the pain that shoots through my face. "Come on." He opens his mouth, his fangs flashing in the light, and sinks them into his wrist before bringing it to my mouth. My lips close around the wound without hesitation, and I swallow a mouthful of his blood, then another, and the pain filling my entire body starts to ebb away. Moments later, it's gone completely. He pulls his arm back, and I reach up to touch my face and find there to be no pain there. I can see clearly from both eyes and my wounds are completely healed.*

*I shake my head. "I'll never get over that."*

*James grins at me, offering me a hand up. "Let's get out of here, yeah?"*

*I can't agree fast enough—I'm very much ready to leave this place.*

*We slip back into the loud room; everyone is dancing and drinking as if nothing happened, and we move along the edge of the room to a side door, which James pushes open to an alleyway next* to the building. I see the others waiting for us at the opening and start toward them with James at my side.

We're about halfway to the street when an angry voice shouts from behind us. Before I can turn, a gunshot cuts through the air. It rings in my ears, vibrating through my skull as fire spreads through my chest. I glance down to find my gray button-up turning red. My head spins, and I reach to touch the redness growing on my shirt. I think I hear Marianne shout my name just before my legs give out and I sink to my knees, falling onto my side as it becomes impossible to breathe. My cheek is pressed against the cold, wet pavement, and my vision blurs with tears as blood spills out of my mouth.

The faces of my friends fade in and out above me.

Will pulls me into his lap and holds my head steady. His voice is muffled when he says, "You're okay. You're going to be fine."

Except, I'm not. I'm dying.

"I gave him my blood, Will," James speaks up.

"I know that," he says in a low voice. "So he's going to be all right."

Sophia meets my gaze. "You can let go, Kade," she says in a soft voice. "We'll be here to help you when you wake." She and Marianne take each of my hands and hold onto me as my eyes close, putting an end to my mortal life.

## 16

## CALLA

"You died because you were sticking up for your friend." I reach out and pry the empty glass from his hand before he shatters it, setting it on the table and pulling my chair closer. "You didn't deserve what happened to you, but your death was a noble one, if that makes you feel any better."

Shit, that sounded so lame. I want to take it back until he offers me a faint smile.

"It turned out okay," he says, "but it sucked for a while."

I nod in understanding. "Are you still in contact with those vampires?"

Kade shrugs. "For a while. We grew apart when I met Lex and Atlas, but we do touch base every decade or so. Marianne and Sophia ended up getting married. They live in Italy right now, I believe. James prides himself on being an eternal bachelor. He travels a lot, so I'm not sure where he is these days."

"What about the other guy? Will?"

I nod. "Will fell in love with a human about thirty years ago. They got married, and he turned her."

"Where are they now?"

He lowers his gaze, frowning. "Marianne contacted me last year and let me know they'd been killed by hunters."

My eyes widen as my stomach sinks. "Shit, Kade. I'm so sorry to hear that."

He nods. "I've gotten used to losing people. When you live forever, that's just part of the adjustment. Granted, it's a bit harder when you lose people who were also meant to live forever." Shadows cloud his face, and I know he's thinking about Meredith again.

I reach for him once more and slide my fingers through his. Standing, I push my chair in and wait for him to do the same before I guide him out of the dining room, and we walk hand-in-hand to his bedroom.

Kade walks over to the bed and drops onto the end of it with a sigh. He drops his chin to his chest, his palms flat against his thighs. "You don't need to hang out with me," he says in a low voice. "If you want—"

"What I want," I cut him off gently, approaching the bed and stopping in front of him, "is to be here for you." I run my fingers through his hair and smile when he finally looks up at me. "Now, come on. I think you could probably use a bit more sleep." I sure as hell could. "Lift your arms."

He arches a brow at me but eventually does, and I pull his shirt off. I point to his pants. "You want to sleep in those?"

"If you want me naked, all you have to do is ask." The words are definitely something I'm used to Kade saying, but his tone is distant. He's trying to put on a strong face but he's really hurting. There's a deep struggle in his eyes that makes my chest ache.

I try to play along, offering him a brilliantly fake smile. "You caught me. Please, oh please, take your pants off."

He shoots me a tired smile, leaning back on the bed to undo his pants and wiggle out of them. Once he's left in just his boxers, he sits up, and I walk around the bed, pulling back the sheets. He follows my movement and gets up, coming to my side and sliding under the sheets.

I wait for Kade to get settled before I go to the other side and undress, keeping only my shirt and panties on before crawling in beside him. I wrap my arms around his waist, pressing my cheek to his bare chest. I close my eyes against the warmth of his skin, listening to the steady beat of his heart as his breathing evens out.

"Thank you," he murmurs, fading into a place where the harsh reality of his life can't reach him, and I hold him tighter as he falls asleep in my arms.

࿐

I wake to the smell of two of my favorite things: coffee and bacon. And then I realize my legs are tangled with Kade's, bringing a rush of warmth to my cheeks and much, much lower. He's still sound asleep, so I'm careful not to move and disturb him. I hold my breath when he shifts slightly, and my eyes widen when his erection presses into my thigh. I close my eyes, trying my best to ignore the rush of heat between my legs—not to mention the throbbing there.

Kade nuzzles his face between my neck and shoulder, making me shiver. I keep my eyes shut and lay my hand over his heart, letting him know I'm here with him. I suck in a breath when his fangs scrape my skin.

"Good morning," I force out in a soft voice.

"Mmm," he breathes against my skin.

I press my lips together, hesitating a moment before tilting my head to give him clear access. "It's okay," I tell him. "Go ahead."

Instead of sinking his fangs into my neck as I'm expecting him to, he kisses the spot just below my ear. "Thank you, but in this state, I'm afraid of how easy it would be to lose control, and I… I don't want to hurt you."

I open my mouth to tell him I trust him but stop myself, nodding. I'm not entirely sure I *do* trust him, especially right now. He's hurt, on edge, and even he's not confident in his ability to control himself. "Blood bag it is. Let's go eat."

We get dressed and head to the kitchen, where we find Gabriel making breakfast. The island is covered with platters of eggs, bacon, hash browns, pancakes, and fresh berries.

My stomach growls, and I don't waste any time finding a plate and loading it up with food. I plop down at the end of the table in the adjoining dining room where Lex is already eating, and Gabriel sets a steaming cup of coffee in front of me. "Thanks," I murmur around a mouthful of scrambled eggs, and he smiles at me.

Kade comes in with a piece of bacon hanging out of his mouth, a plate with more bacon in one hand, and a tall glass of blood in the other. He sits next to Lex, who throws his arm around Kade's shoulders briefly before returning his attention to the food in front of him.

Gabriel joins us a few minutes later, and we eat in silence.

I'm the one to break it several moments later when I ask, "What's going to happen once the vampires start their attack on the hunters? Won't that ignite a full-on war?"

Atlas chooses that moment to waltz into the room, holding his phone and a coffee cup. "It'll depend on how the hunters around the globe respond to the initial attack." He sits at the other end of the table, setting his phone down and taking a drink. "It's essentially a reminder of which species is more resilient and powerful. The hunters have been around nearly as long as we have, and there are blips in history where their presence is more pronounced—like now, for instance—but that will change, as it always does."

I frown at the onslaught of information. "So history is just going to continue repeating itself?"

"It's more complicated than that, angel," Gabriel says in a gentle tone, lifting a forkful of hash browns to his mouth.

"I don't think it is," I argue. "You're reminding the humans where they—*we*—hang on the food chain. There's nothing complicated about that." Disappointing as hell, sure, but not complicated.

I don't know what else to say—there really isn't anything else *to* say. It's out of my hands and even Atlas's, I figure.

Clearing my throat, I stand, pushing my chair back and grabbing my dishes to take to the sink. "I'm going to get some air."

A quick trip to the bathroom, and I'm ready for a run. Physical activity has always helped me to clear my mind, and the sun is shining brightly this morning, which I'm hoping will improve my mood.

I walk out to the hallway, scrolling on my phone to find a good playlist, and stop abruptly at the sensation of someone moving past me at an inhuman speed. I exhale a heavy breath, lifting my gaze to find Atlas blocking the front door with his arms crossed over his chest.

My eyes narrow, and I take another step forward, slipping my phone into the pocket of my leggings.

He shakes his head. "Do not pass GO. Do not collect two hundred dollars."

"He makes jokes now," I comment wryly.

"Oh, I'm very serious. You're not leaving."

"Would you chill? I'm going for a run. You can't keep me locked in here."

His expression darkens, and he lowers his voice. "Want to bet?"

"No," I reply firmly, "I want you to get the fuck out of my way."

"You're not going out there," he says simply, and when I open my mouth to argue, he continues, "It's not safe now that the hunters know you're associated with us."

I blink at him. He's... concerned about me. Or he just wants to hold power over me. Again. "I can't stay cooped up in here, Atlas. I'm going stir crazy. I need to blow off steam." I swallow hard and say the word I absolutely loathe using in conversation with him. "Please?"

He narrows his eyes, glaring at me so long I'm fully expecting him to refuse. But then he says, "Fine. I'll go with you."

That's kind of the opposite of helpful, considering I was going to get my mind *off* the vampires, but I suppose I should take what I can get.

"Great," I deadpan, sticking my headphones in and cranking up the music on my phone as we walk out the front door.

We start at a light jog, and my feet hitting against the sidewalk in time with my slightly accelerated heartbeat makes me feel significantly better than sitting at the dining room table discussing the impending vampire hunter war. And yet, I'm still thinking about it. What it'll mean for me and the guys, Brighton and her family... I change the song on my phone and pick up my pace, trying to drown out my thoughts. That, and ignore the vampire easily keeping pace beside me. As hard as I pretend he's not there, I can't help but feel him all over.

I give my head a shake as we round the corner and pick up speed again. There's a park ahead with what looks to be a walking trail, so I set my sights on it, my feet pounding the pavement and gravel through the park until we hit the dirt path. I slow my pace a little in case we run into other people, but Atlas evidently doesn't share that concern. Between one moment and the next, he grabs me around the waist and hauls me off the trail into the forest, knocking my headphones out in the process.

"Atlas! What the hell?" My heartbeat pounds in my throat and my vision blurs with the inhuman movement until my back hits the hard bark of a tree. I immediately start fighting him, throwing my arms out and shoving as hard as I can. It does virtually nothing besides exert my already low energy.

"Enough," he says, gripping my wrists in one of his hands and lifting them over my head.

I glare at him, my chest heaving between us. "What are you doing? Is this our thing now?"

His lips twitch for a split second. "You'd like that, wouldn't you?" His eyes glimmer. "If I took you against this tree and fucked you so hard you couldn't walk back to the house."

I swallow past the dryness in my throat. "You'd look pretty funny having to carry me back there."

Atlas leans in until his nose grazes mine. "Perhaps a risk I'm willing to take."

"Like giving a shit about human life?" I blurt.

He pulls back, his brows knitting as he lets my wrists go. "What?"

My pulse kicks up, but I don't attempt to move away. I have no idea what I'm doing, but with everything going on, I feel as if I'm spiraling, desperate for something concrete to hold onto. "Do your parents know you care about a human?"

He grasps my shoulders, not holding me against the tree anymore, just holding me. "Why are you asking me that?"

"You have to do what they say, that was made clear to me with what's been planned for the hunters." I drop my gaze, staring at the brush at our feet. "I guess I'm just wondering what'll happen when it comes to what they want you to do with me."

"They're indifferent to our arrangement." His grip on my

shoulders loosens. "It's not something they're concerned about, Calla."

I say nothing, but my pulse is still pounding from running—and being this close to Atlas. I guess I hadn't realized just how worried I was about Atlas's parents and what they thought about their son's... whatever I am. I've been so tangled up with worry over Kade and Brighton I didn't really consider what it all meant for *me*—until now, apparently.

His eyes dance across my face, and when I turn away, he drops one hand from my shoulder and snags my chin, forcing my gaze back to his. "You're safe. They aren't..." He sighs, lowering his voice to something so calm and soft, it's almost unrecognizable. "I'm not going to let anyone bring harm to you."

My chest tightens, and I hold his gaze. "Okay," I finally say.

His thumb brushes over my jaw. "We should get back. I don't like being out in the open like this." He steps back, giving me space, then we walk back to the trail before picking up the pace and jogging toward the house.

I walk up the front steps ahead of him and reach for the door. Before my hand can wrap around the handle, Atlas pulls me back and spins me around. I don't have a moment's warning before his lips are on mine. His arm snakes around me, hauling me against him as his mouth devours mine in an all-consuming, world-narrowing kiss.

For a brief time, we're just two people losing ourselves to each other. It's incredible and awful, and I want nothing more than to pretend it'll last forever.

Something in me cracks as fear digs its claws deep into my chest. I never wanted this—I dreaded the day the vampires would come for me—and now, all I can think about is how scared I am to lose them.

I break the kiss, leaning my forehead against his jaw while I catch my breath. "I need to ask you something."

"So ask."

"Would you stay out of the attack if I asked?" Now that I don't have to worry about Brighton's safety, that leaves plenty of room for concern over the guys. I'm not sure if the others are expected to participate, but Atlas definitely is.

He leans back as his eyes roam over my face. "Worried about me?"

"Don't answer a question with a question," I grumble.

"Well, we're not close enough to drive to Washington in time anyway, so I guess I'll sit it out." A flight would give him plenty of time to be there for tonight, but I'm not about to offer that up. I'd be telling him something he already knows, anyway.

"Will that get you in trouble?" I ask in a quiet voice. Everything I've heard about Atlas's parents makes me hope I never have the misfortune of meeting them.

The corner of his mouth quirks. "I think the ability to be grounded becomes a little less effective after you've lived for over a hundred years."

I shoot him a look. "I'm so glad you can find humor in this."

"You'd be smart to as well. Otherwise, this is going to get very dark, very fast."

*Too fucking late.*

## 17

## KADE

None of us slept longer than a few hours last night. When Atlas and Calla got back from their outing —and sucking each other's faces on the front porch while Lex and I watched from the living room—we passed the time watching shitty reality television in the insane theater downstairs. Lex ordered enough pizza and wings for an army, and the four of us stuffed our faces. Atlas took his time eating a single slice, I think mostly to have something to do with his hands. We were all antsy and on edge, having decided to stay away from Washington and any of the other hunter attacks that took place simultaneously last night.

Sitting together in the living room, we wait for Atlas's phone to ring, for one of his contacts from New York to brief us on the stats of the attack.

Calla's asleep in one of the bedrooms; Gabriel suggested there was no sense waking her until we had information to offer, and we agreed with him.

My phone chimes from the coffee table, and I lean forward on the couch enough to see Marcel's name on the text alert. I swipe it up and scan the message. It's short and to the point, just like Marcel.

"The Washington house has been cleaned out and rented," I announce to the guys, my shoulders feeling heavier than they did moments ago. That place was home to us. We had it built from designs Atlas created. It's another loss I can't seem to accept.

"How long is the lease?" Lex asks, frowning.

"Marcel didn't say." I shrug. "Probably a year."

Gabriel says nothing. He continues staring out the front window in thought, one leg crossed over the other.

What I wouldn't give to know the thoughts in his head right now.

"It doesn't matter," Atlas says, taking a drink from his mug. If I didn't have heightened senses, I'd think he was drinking coffee, but the thick, coppery scent of blood makes my nostrils flare.

Lex nods, kicking his legs up on the coffee table. "You're right. Whenever we're ready to go back, Marcel will take care of it. Glamour whoever's in there to pack up their shit and get the fuck out."

He's not wrong. Still, the thought of someone else living in *our* home makes my hands ball into fists. We wouldn't be in this mess if it weren't for the hunters.

Gabriel wets his lips, reaching into his pocket when his phone chimes. "It's Fallon. They went to Chicago after leaving us and they spotted Selene last night." He types a message back, then tells us, "I've asked them to keep tabs on her until we can get there. I don't want them taking her on themselves."

"Good. We deserve the pleasure of ending her miserable existence," I say in a sharp tone. I'm itching to shed some blood. Anything to sate the angry demon making a home in my chest.

Atlas is next to pull out his phone and stares hard at the screen. Before he can tell us what's going on, Calla shuffles into the room still in the black T-shirt and sweatpants she fell asleep in, rubbing the sleep from her eyes.

Fucking hell. I immediately want to tug her into my lap and bury my face in her neck. My cock twitches in my pants, and I grit my teeth. Now is *not* the time.

"Any news?" she asks around a yawn, dropping onto the couch next to me and hugging her knees to her chest as her tired gaze moves between us.

"Just now," Atlas says, and we all turn our attention to him. He clears his throat. "My advisors from Chicago and New York report that nearly fifty vampires were killed during the raids last night. Dozens more were injured but are now fully recovered after feeding."

Calla gasps softly at his words and wraps her arms around her legs, her brows pinching together. She's conflicted. Here she sits as a human in a room full of vampires while we talk about other vampires killing humans. The worst ones, the ones who want to kill *us*, but still. I understand what must be going through her head, because when I thought Meredith betrayed me, I still couldn't find it in me to hate her, to not *not* want to know her, given the chance.

"And the hunters?" Gabriel asks. "How many were lost?"

"Lost?" Lex says with a bitter laugh. "Ain't no loss, brother."

Gabriel sighs. "You know what I mean."

"At least three hundred," Atlas says. "We don't have final numbers yet, but it's predicted that number will climb as the day goes on."

"What about Scott?" Calla asks in a small voice, her pulse ticking faster with each passing minute.

"I can't confirm either way at this point," Atlas tells her.

"I'm in touch with the team in Washington, so I'll know more soon."

With a short nod, she gets up and walks to the kitchen, where I can hear her getting a mug out of the cupboard and pouring herself some coffee.

"Well, I can't just sit around here all day," I say, getting off the couch. I noticed a pool in the backyard when we arrived, so I head outside into the sun, tugging my shirt off and losing my pants before diving into the water. Swimming laps back and forth across the pool, I focus myself on the movement of my arms, kicking hard, while remaining at a human pace. My muscles won't tire like they would when I was human, but the exertion is still a decent distraction. Until an even better one walks out the back door onto the deck with a steaming mug in her hands and walks toward the pool.

"I didn't even notice this place had a pool," she says, dropping onto one of the lounge chairs and taking a sip of her coffee.

I swim to the edge closest to her, propping my arms on the concrete lip of the pool. "Are you planning to sit there and watch or are you going to come in this time?"

Her cheeks turn pink as she presumably recalls the day at our house in the pool when I feasted between her lovely thighs.

"I…" She glances down at her clothes. "I don't have a suit."

The corner of my mouth kicks up. "Hmm. I'll give you one chance to guess what I'm wearing."

She rolls her eyes. "I'm not jumping in there naked, Kade. Nice try."

"Why not?" I push, gliding away from the edge and back as she watches me.

Calla gestures around. "Uh, what if someone sees?"

"Someone like who? Gabriel?" I add with a faint smirk,

rather enjoying this moment being so reminiscent of the last time we were near a pool together.

Her cheeks flush hotter, and she shakes her head. "This place might feel secluded, but it's still fairly suburban."

I let out a heavy sigh. "Fine. Be like that. I suppose I'll just keep swimming laps to try to keep myself occupied."

She sets her mug on the deck next to her chair and pins me with a half-hearted glare. "Are you trying to get me in the pool with pity?"

I shrug. "Is it working?"

Holding my gaze for a stretch of silence, she blows out a breath and stands, tugging her sweatpants down until they fall to her ankles. She steps out of them and kicks them aside, then walks closer to the pool, crossing her arms over her chest.

"Come on," I encourage. "The water is nice and refreshing."

She chews her bottom lip, glancing back toward the house for a second before turning back to me and moving to sit at the edge, dipping her feet then her legs into the pool.

I swim to her, sliding my hands up her bare legs and holding her gaze as I reach her panties. "Are these coming off?"

Her gaze lowers as if she's trying to see what I'm wearing, and I can't help but chuckle. Her eyes find mine once more, and she presses her lips together. My hands go to her waist, soaking her T-shirt as I pull her toward me and into the pool, deciding I'd rather let her make the move to undress then guide her into doing it.

She grabs my shoulders, her breath hitching as I lower her into the water. She slowly relaxes as her feet touch the bottom and the water soaks through her shirt. She leans into me, gliding her fingers through my hair and resting her forehead against mine. "So, what? We're just going to distract each other with sex in the pool of a stranger's house?" Her voice is soft, barely above a whisper, but I catch every word.

Nodding, I slide my hands around to cup her ass and press her against my cock beneath the water. "Any objections?"

Her pulse races, and she lifts her chin, sealing her lips with mine.

*Message fucking received.*

I kiss her hard, closing my eyes and losing myself to the feel of her against me. She makes a soft noise that goes straight to my dick, and I squeeze her ass, lifting her up so she can wrap her legs around me.

Our lips battle for control, and I tear her panties clean off, tossing them onto the deck, and she yelps against my lips. *So much for waiting for her to undress.* My teeth catch her bottom lip, and I nip it gently, keeping my fangs retracted even as she grinds against me, tempting the monster just below the surface.

"Kade," she moans, leaning back to catch her breath.

I turn us around and pin her against the side of the pool, kissing the tip of her nose. "Tell me," I murmur, "would you like me to fuck you with my fingers, my tongue, or my cock?"

Her eyes are filled with hunger and her lips curve into a smile she doesn't try to hide. "You're making me choose?" She flicks her tongue over her bottom lip. "What if I want all three?"

I press my lips to hers in a chaste kiss, then dip my hand between her thighs, tracing along her slit with two fingers. "I'll give you anything you desire, Calla. Never doubt that for a second." I push inside her at the same moment I capture her mouth again, reveling in her warmth, in the taste of her lips, and when she kisses me back, grinding herself on my fingers, I'm about to lose my fucking mind with the need to bury my cock between her thighs.

She grips the back of my hair, moving her lips with mine as her heart thumps in her chest. I circle her clit with my thumb for good measure, picking up the pace of my fingers and curling them to hit the spot that'll drive her wild. Her pussy clenches around my fingers, and my cock throbs in response, my balls tightening.

"I need more," she murmurs against my lips, and holy hell, it's so sexy I couldn't deny her if I wanted to; she doesn't need glamour to control me.

I pull my fingers out, making her shiver with delight, and tweak her clit before lining my cock up with her entrance. I tease her with the blunt head, and her chest rises and falls quickly as she stares into my eyes, pleading. I push inside her all the way in one smooth thrust, her pussy already wet enough to allow me to glide in easily. I groan, completely sheathed in her heat, and give her a few seconds to catch her breath before I start to pull out slowly.

She grabs my hip, holding me inside her. "You feel so good." Her voice is low and breathy and her cheeks are flushed beautifully; I'd like nothing more than to have this vision of her etched into my mind permanently.

Pressure fills my chest at the thought. I never want to let this stubborn as hell, sharp-tongued, and unbelievably compassionate human go. She is very easily the best thing to happen to me—to any of us, I think. And I very much intend to show her that.

I roll my hips, pushing in deeper, and she presses her lips together, her eyes fluttering shut as her face fills with the most serene expression. She slides her hand from my hip to my ass, digging her fingers into my skin, and I in turn pick up the pace of my thrusts, pounding into her until we're both breathing heavily. Her pussy clenches around me, and I steal her mouth as she cries out in pleasure, kissing her as she squeezes my cock, soaking it with her release. My muscles tighten and the most delicious pressure fills me just before my climax crests and I come hard, filling her with my release as she moans, riding the aftershocks of her orgasm.

Our lips part, and we catch our breaths, but I make no move to pull out of her heat. I kiss each of her cheeks, then her forehead.

"I've never had sex in a pool before," she murmurs with a soft laugh.

I chuckle, tucking her hair behind her ear and tweaking her chin. "Glad I was your first."

"Mmm. Do you plan to stay buried between my thighs for the rest of the day, or…?" There's a playful glint in her eyes that I can't help but grin at.

"Perhaps," I taunt, dipping my face to kiss her again, slow and deep, until her pulse is racing once more. I lean back, flicking my eyes between hers. "As much as I'd like to, we should probably head back inside and see what's going on."

Her smile fades quickly, and she nods. "Okay, fine. But you know, you fucked me with your fingers and your cock." She lowers her voice, pressing her chest against mine. "But I didn't get your tongue."

My cock twitches inside her, and I smirk. "Oh, I'm well aware. I'm saving my dessert for later."

Her pussy clenches around me again, and she pulls in an unsteady breath.

"Come on," I say, sliding my cock out and guiding her to the other side of the pool closest to the house. I jump out, then turn and offer her my hand. She takes it, and I pull her up, her T-shirt clinging to her and making her nipples stand out. Fuck. I already want her again.

*Later*, I vow to myself. Something tells me I'm going to need something to look forward to.

## ❧ 18 ❧

## CALLA

I leave Kade's side when we return to the house and head upstairs to the bathroom across the hall from where I've been sleeping. Turning on the shower, I peel off my wet T-shirt, dropping it into the sink and catching my flushed complexion in the antique, gold-framed mirror over the marble vanity. My cheeks and chest are tinged pink and my hair's a mess of tangles and saltwater from the pool. Besides that, though, I look… happy. Which feels all kinds of wrong considering everything going on around me, but I suppose I should be grateful that I can experience some goodness even with shit hitting the fan.

After my shower, I tug on a clean pair of black leggings and an oversized sweater. My stomach grumbles as I'm yanking a brush through my wet hair. Evidently I worked up quite the appetite in the pool.

I'm about to go downstairs to start making something for lunch when my phone starts vibrating from the bedside table. I walk over, and when I see Brighton's name on the screen, I snatch it up and answer it. "Tell me you're okay," I say quickly.

"Your concern for my daughter is meaningless when you choose to spend your time with monsters, Calla."

*Scott.*

So he wasn't killed during the raids.

"Where is Brighton?" I say with an edge to my voice. There goes my appetite.

"Brighton," he says, "is not who you should be worried about."

My hand curls into a fist at my side as I start pacing the bedroom. "What the hell does that mean?"

"Choices have consequences." His voice is level and calm.

A surge of anger flares through me in response. "You have no idea what you're talking about," I say through my teeth, clenching my jaw. I'm not about to tell him about the blood oath, that my being with the vampires was never a *choice*. I have a feeling it wouldn't really matter to him at this point, anyway. "What do you want, Scott?"

"Personally, I want nothing. My organization, however—"

"If this is a recruitment call, you're wasting your breath," I cut in.

He laughs. "Noted. It's a shame, though. You certainly have a fire that would make you a strong candidate."

"I'm hanging up now," I practically growl into the phone.

"You'd be wise to consider your options, Calla. *You* may be safe for now, but what of the others you care for?"

My stomach drops and ice fills my veins. "What did you just say?"

The line goes dead.

"Fuck," I shout at the empty room. Storming to the door, I rip it open and rush downstairs.

Kade and Gabriel aren't around, but Lex and Atlas are sitting at the dining room table, drinking blood from tall crystal glasses. They both turn to look at me when I burst into the room, out of breath.

"Calla?" Lex says, arching a brow at me.

"He's alive," I force out, swallowing hard. "Scott is alive, and I… I think he threatened me. I don't know—he hung up on me before I could get him to elaborate."

Lex's fangs flash in the light over the table, and he gets to his feet in a flash. "He won't be alive for long."

"Lex," Atlas says in a deep voice, "take a beat." His sharp eyes focus on me as he stands. "Tell me exactly what he said."

I rehash the short conversation, clenching my phone in my hand. "What the fuck am I supposed to do with that?"

"We'll handle it," Atlas tells me, lines of tension creasing between his brows.

My phone goes off again, and my pulse jumps. Atlas pries it out of my hand easily before I can catch a glance at the screen, and when I reach for it, he holds it away from me.

"It's your father," he says.

My heart stops. "Give it to me."

Instead of heeding my demand, Atlas answers the call, lifting my phone to his ear. I try to grab it from him, but he turns away, and Lex catches my wrist, pulling me toward him.

"Mr. Montgomery," Atlas says in a smooth voice, "what can I do for you?"

I look between Lex and Atlas, knowing Lex can hear the call just as clearly as Atlas can, while I'm left in the dark. "What's going on?" I ask.

Lex frowns but says nothing, freeing my wrist from his grip.

Atlas turns, meeting my gaze and nodding. "I understand. Let me speak with her, and we'll sort things out." He ends the call, setting my phone on the table.

"I haven't spoken to my father in over a month." My voice sounds hollow. "What is going on?" I demand. "What the hell happened?"

Gabriel and Kade slip into the room, concern etched on their faces, and I know something is very wrong.

"Your mom was in an accident. Someone blew through a red light and hit her. She's in surgery now. Your father couldn't tell me anything more."

I stare at his face, my throat too thick to force any words out. My chin trembles and my vision blurs with hot tears. Without warning, my legs give out, and Lex moves to catch me around the waist before I collapse onto the floor.

"Calla," Gabriel starts.

"No," I croak, tears rolling down my cheeks. I shake my head, my heart thumping so hard in my chest it pulses in my throat. "This isn't happening."

Gabriel steps in front of me, taking up my whole world. "Listen to me, angel. We're going to get in the car right now. We'll be in New York in an hour."

I get the feeling back in my legs enough to stand on my own and wipe the tears from my cheeks. "He did this," I say in a shallow tone. "Scott told me the people I care about weren't safe. I didn't think... How could this have happened?"

"He must've had someone set up to cause the accident at his direction," Kade comments, his arms crossed over his chest where he leans in the doorway, his expression as murderous as I feel right now.

"We don't know for sure that it's related," Lex offers. "Sure, it looks like it, but it's New York. Dozens of car accidents happen every hour."

I shake my head. Deep in my gut, I know this isn't a coincidence. The hunters did this.

My mom could die because of the hunter's war with the vampires.

The hospital lights are bright, and my nose burns with the harsh scent of antiseptic in the air as I charge toward the information desk inside the triage center. We find out my mom is out of surgery, and I start crying again because she made it through the procedure—*she's alive.*

After what feels like the longest elevator ride of my life, we reach the surgical recovery floor, and I nearly throw myself off the elevator and sprint toward her room, my Docs smacking the shiny white tiles as I weave in between hospital staff.

I skid to a stop outside her room, suddenly frozen, unable to move my feet to step inside.

My dad looks up from the chair he's in across the room, and his bloodshot eyes fill with tears as he gets to his feet and comes toward me.

"Dad?" I whisper, silent tears rolling down my cheeks.

"Come here, sweetheart." He wraps his arms around me, holding me as sobs tear through me, and I cling to him, the pressure in my chest finally exploding.

"Is she going to be okay?" I ask after getting the sobs under control. I glance past him to where the curtain is pulled over so I can only see the lower half of her body, which is covered in blankets.

"She pulled through the surgery, but she hasn't woken up yet. The doctors said it could take some time, so we just need to try and be patient." He runs his hand down my hair, tucking it back. "Did you come alone?"

I shake my head, sniffling. "They're in the hall," I say in a low voice.

His jaw clenches as disgust fills his expression.

"Dad, please. Just forget about that right now."

He pulls me into another hug, then guides me over to the bed.

I suck in a short breath at the sight of my mom hooked up

to too many machines to count. There's an oxygen mask over her mouth and nose, IVs connected to both arms, and bandages covering several areas of her arms, face, and chest.

"Calla," my dad says in a soft voice.

I force my eyes away from Mom. "Why did she need surgery?"

He frowns, hesitating as if he doesn't want to tell me. "She had some internal bleeding and a punctured lung, which is what required the surgery. They inserted a chest tube, so she'll be here a while when she wakes, but you know your mom. She's stubborn. I know she'll make it out of this."

We sit around her bed, and I take her hand, holding it between both of mine.

Hours pass. Nurses come and go, checking over the machines and even bringing me a blanket at one point.

I'm not sure where the guys are. Half of me wishes they were by my side, but the other half is glad they're not. I don't have the mental capacity to think about that right now, so I don't even try.

Sometime after dinner, I send my dad home to change and eat a proper meal.

I must have dozed off, because I open my eyes to find a woman in a white coat standing at the end of the bed, looking over my mom's file.

"Sorry to wake you," she says in a gentle voice, offering me a kind smile.

I sit up, wiping my eyes, and shake my head. "It's fine. How is she?"

The doctor's smile slips a little. "Usually by this point, we start to see some improvement, but there's nothing yet."

My mouth goes dry. "What does that mean?"

"She's in a coma." Her tone is soft, but her words shoot ice through my chest.

I stare at the woman, then snatch the file out of her hands

as if I'm going to be able to make sense of what's inside. "But she's going to wake up, right?"

"Her body needs time to heal. That could take days or weeks, maybe longer."

"You didn't answer my question," I say, dropping my eyes to the file in my hands. I flip through the pages. They aren't just records of this hospital stay. I come across the one from five years ago when Mom had brutal kidney stones, then the documentation from my birth.

"We'll continue to monitor her," the doctor says as I continue thumbing through Mom's file.

My eyes catch on another hospital stay a few years before I was born. I squint at the words, sure I'm reading them wrong. This must be a mistake. Something from someone else's records that was misfiled.

"What is this?"

The doctor sighs. "I really shouldn't be allowing you to see that. Medical records are—"

"What is this?" I repeat, shoving the file back at her.

She scans the page and frowns. "Oh. Your mom was admitted for a delivery, but unfortunately, it looks like the child didn't survive."

I blink at her, my thoughts spinning and moving too fast to string together anything coherent for almost a minute. "She had a baby before me," I say to myself.

"Yes. I'm sorry, you shouldn't have seen that. I'd think if your mom wanted you to know about the child, she would have shared it with you."

Something clicks, and the words fly out of my mouth before I can think to stop them. "Was the baby alive when it was delivered?"

She frowns, dropping her gaze to the file once more. She flips a couple of pages and nods. "According to the death certificate, she lived a few hours."

*She.*

Oh my god.

My world narrows. Black dances around the edges of my vision and my heart slams against my chest.

"S-she?" I whisper. "My mom had a baby girl before I was born?"

The doctor nods. I watch her mouth move, but I can't hear anything over the ringing in my ears.

*I wasn't the firstborn Montgomery daughter.*

Whatever debt my ancestors owed to the vampires—the blood oath was never mine to fulfill.

## END OF BOOK THREE

READ BOOK FOUR NOW! mybook.to/fatedinruby!

If you enjoyed *Entangled in Scarlet*, please leave a review on Amazon and Goodreads. Reviews are so important for authors to find new readers!

Sign up for the newsletter at www.authorjacarter.com/newsletter-sign-up for book news!

Join J.A. Carter on Patreon at www.patreon.com/authorjacarter for exclusive access to signed paperbacks, bonus content, early cover reveals and book releases, plus so much more!

Follow J.A. Carter on Instagram and TikTok (@authorjacarter) to stay up to date with all of the things!

Join J.A. Carter's Reader Lounge on Facebook for first looks and exclusives!

# ACKNOWLEDGMENTS

Thank you, thank you, thank you to everyone who has joined me on this wild ride so far. I can't wait for you to find out what Calla and the guys are in for... ;)

And a huge shoutout to my beta readers: Ty, Haileigh, Jennifer, Charlotte, Ashley, Kylee, and Carolyn—you are amazing and your feedback was so helpful and encouraging, I can't thank you enough!

xx,
    J.A. Carter